STRONG

NATALIE DEBRABANDERE

Disclaimer:

Please bear in mind that this is a work of fiction, and as such I have
allowed myself a certain amount of creative license regarding military
rules and regulations. This means that sometimes I may have bent the
rules a little, in order to accommodate my story.
I apologise in advance for any significant mistakes.

ISBN: 1491220988
ISBN-13: 978-1491220986

DEDICATION

To the lovely people who read my first novel, Unbroken, and took
the time to write really wonderful reviews online.
Also dedicated to the exceptional people who serve in the military, in
the United States and the UK, and who inspired me to write the
story of Kate and Tyler. Thank you so much guys.

PART ONE

Chapter One

Cobel FOB, Helmand, Afghanistan.
September 2012.

Combat Medic Kate Sanderson steadied herself for what she knew would be a typically rough landing in hostile territory. As the black Army Chinook she was on started its descent, it dropped fast and hard in sudden bursts. It was heart in your mouth kind of stuff, pretty good simulation for a textbook crash. Also standard practice in these parts, and nothing to worry about at all. As a general rule, Kate enjoyed flying, and she also had absolute confidence in the talented pilots who flew the Chinooks out there in Afghanistan.

But she dreaded these tactical landings and knew she always would.

Of course she understood that the manoeuvre was necessary in order to reduce the amount of time the helicopter would be exposed to enemy fire, if any. Unfortunately knowing the reason behind it did not make it any less unpleasant, and already she could feel her stomach beginning to twist and roll.

She allowed herself a quick glance out of the tiny window on her left but could see nothing but darkness. She returned her gaze forward very quickly and concentrated on breathing deep and slow, the way she knew worked for her, reminding herself that they would be on the ground soon and trying to keep her stomach from crawling up inside her mouth. In front of her several large plastic crates crammed with equipment, food and ammunition blocked her view of much of the inside of the machine.

Kate was using a scheduled re-supply drop to the outpost as her entry ticket to Cobel, and the reason they were using a Chinook was that the area around the Forward Operating Base was heavily mined. Flying was safer than driving a truck, even an armoured one, even in the middle of the night.

"Ten seconds!" the loadmaster shouted in her direction.

Apart from him and his buddy she was the only one on board in the back, and she gave them both a thumbs up and a quick smile.

Leaning forward a little, she shouldered her heavy Bergen, ready to get out as quickly as she could. She had practiced this sort of thing many times before, in training and on operations, and she knew the Chinook would not stay on the ground for very long regardless of how much time it took her to get going. Even so, there was no way she would be able to run out very fast, not with the amount of weight she was carrying on her back.

With her ammunition, clothes, webbing, weapons, and various bits and pieces of equipment, her bag weighed close to 60 kilograms.

Almost her own body weight in gear.

She did not have time to think about that for very long though. The ramp dropped even before the heavy machine was fully on the ground, and Kate braced herself.

With her combat goggles safely on, she staggered out into a whirlwind of grit, gravel and sand, wincing a little as she felt its sharp sting on her cheeks and mouth. She made sure that she got off the ramp quickly though, and without losing her balance. Once she was a safe distance away she dropped down on one knee, breathing a little harder. She shrugged her shoulders to readjust her load more comfortably and tightened her grip on her weapon, squinting through all the dust hanging in the air as she tried to make sense of her surroundings.

Behind her the crates got unloaded in the blink of an eye, and the helicopter was gone less than ten seconds after landing. In the deep silence that followed, Kate glanced to her left and spotted the compound, about fifty meters away.

It was two in the morning, deep into enemy territory. Kate's new posting was twelve weeks attached to a company of US Marines at Cobel, and she had been travelling for nearly two days to get to it. From the familiar safety of RAF Brize Norton in the UK, on to Kandahar, then Bastion, and finally Cobel. She felt a little spaced out, almost hung over. It did not help that her eyes had not adjusted to the darkness yet, and she felt very on edge about being out in the open in what she knew to be such a dangerous place.

Fortunately, just as her heart was beginning to race a little, she spotted movement on her right and one of the marines she had expected to see suddenly stepped forward out of the shadows to meet her.

He grabbed her hand and shook it, and she relaxed a little. She was glad to see him, glad to see how confident and at ease he appeared to be.

"Doctor Sanderson?"

"Sergeant," she replied with a quick nod.

"Welcome to Cobel. The boss is out on patrol so I'll get you settled in. Just walk right behind me. Make sure you stay on the path."

Kate gave him a thumbs up. She knew the drill. Even this close to the compound the troops were taking no chances with potential

IEDs, and Kate was well aware that hidden bombs would be a constant threat over the next few weeks. Unfortunately, probably also the main cause of injury to the soldiers she was about to join at Cobel.

"Got it, let's go," she said.

Apart from the occasional comment from her guide on their team radio, everybody was quiet as they made their way quickly back toward the compound, and after a couple of minutes they slipped inside the secure area, through a narrow hole in the wall well-guarded by a couple of sentries.

"Here we go doctor, home sweet home," the tall gunner announced.

Kate took a deep breath and exhaled slowly.

Safe, she thought. For now.

"Great," she smiled. "Call me Kate."

"Sure thing, Kate."

He stood in front of her and released the straps on his body armour, took his gloves off.

"So how long have you guys been at Cobel now, Sergeant?" Kate asked him.

She lowered her rucksack to the ground and stretched her back. She twisted around a little until she heard it pop, and felt instantly better.

"Just over eight weeks," he replied.

He whipped off his helmet and smiled at her.

"Name's Ben Collins. Welcome to our little bit of front line. It's not much, but we like it."

Kate took a few seconds to look around, a little taken aback at the state of the compound.

Everything seemed to be open ground. The walls were only about three meters high on every side, and made of mud. There were no solid buildings anywhere to be seen on the inside, and Kate had definitely not been expecting that. She could see observation posts at each corner of the compound, equipped with heavy machine guns and mortars which she knew would be manned twenty-four hours a day. Still, she would have preferred solid Hesco walls to this. The term "dump" came to mind, although of course since this was a Marines' camp, a very tidy and organised one…

The soldiers had set up camp on the Western side of the compound as close as possible to the thick mud walls. Probably in case anybody came near enough to throw a grenade inside, Kate suspected, even though it was very unlikely that anyone would manage to get close enough to give that a try.

Tarpaulins and tents, combined with sand bags and remnants of wooden boxes and crates, had all been positioned as creatively and strategically as possible in order to turn this godforsaken place into as much of a home for these marines for the time being. Kate noticed a small stream that snaked its way through the compound, and there was a little pond at the back. She spotted space for a few solar showers nearby as well. A bunch of trees and some bits of wood were clustered around it, giving a slight illusion of privacy.

Collins led her through, stopping when he reached the last tent at the end.

"This is where the boss sleeps," he said, opening up the tent flap for Kate so she could take a quick look inside. "There's a free bed in there for you. She's out on a job with a few of the guys but they should be back just before dawn."

Kate shivered a little.

"Okay, thanks. Is it getting really cold around here or is it just me?" she enquired.

"Gets to be pretty warm during the day still, but yeah, colder at night. Makes a change from all the stupid heat we've had all over the summer, you know? "

He grinned at her, looking relaxed, and Kate returned his smile.

Her last posting, she reflected. It would be fine.

After ten years in the British Medical Corps and tours of duty in Bosnia, Iraq and Afghanistan, she had finally decided that she would leave the army at the end of this campaign. She was thirty-four, five-six, with shiny black hair that just brushed her shoulders when she had it down. A keen rower back at home, she was athletic and muscular looking. She could hold her own with most soldiers when it came to physical fitness.

"I think I should have packed a few more warmers," she commented lightly.

"Hey, don't worry. Any kit you need and didn't bring, the boss will share with you."

"What's her name?" Kate asked.

It was the third time that he had mentioned "the boss", and there was a lot of respect in his voice when he did. Kate was curious.

"Oh, the captain," he said with a quick nod. "Her name's Tyler."

"Right. What is it like working with her?"

Collins looked her straight in the eye and gave a little shrug.

"She's good, I trust her," he said simply. Then he winked at her and laughed. "Don't tell her I said that, hey doc?"

Kate chuckled.

"No worries. How long have you two known each other?"

"Five years. Tyler's solid. Just the sort you want watching your back when you're out there on patrol."

Kate watched in silence as he lit a small Hexy stove and put coffee on the go for the both of them. They sat together for a little while longer, and Collins answered some of Kate's questions about the compound, day to day life, and security at the camp.

"There are forty-eight of us out here, divided into four platoons. We patrol every day," he said. "And at night too. It's important that we make our presence felt."

"Does this camp get targeted often?"

"Used to at first, but not really anymore. We get Taliban observing us from time to time, but there are fewer and fewer of them around."

Kate raised a questioning eyebrow.

"Not many dickers are a match for our snipers," Collins explained with a wry smile.

"I see. And are there many Taliban groups left around this particular area you think?"

"Yeah, we reckon quite a few. Some pose as farmers. Some don't bother. They tend to come and go. We get shot at when we go out sometimes, but with so many of our guys on the ground, and with the firepower that we bring, they know there isn't much they can do to hurt us that way."

"So they lay on IEDs..."

"That they certainly do."

Collins' expression darkened. He stared thoughtfully into his coffee and slowly turned the mug in his hands.

"We lost one of our guys to an IED, first week we were here. Last week two guys from Taliki also got injured and had to be medivaced out. That's only two clicks East," he added. "Guess it's not a matter of "if" it's going to happen, just a matter of when..."

On that sombre comment, he drained the rest of his mug and prepared to stand up.

"If that's all for now ma'am..."

"Kate."

"If that's all for now Kate," he corrected himself with a smile, "I think I'd better go get some sleep before I go out on patrol again."

"Sure. Thanks for the warm welcome Sergeant."

"Ben."

Kate nodded, flashed him a bright smile.

"Ben. See you tomorrow."

After Collins had left, leaving her alone in the tent to organise her few belongings, Kate tried not to think too much about his last comment.

As a professional soldier she knew the risks, they all did. She did her best to stay safe and make sure that those around her were safe as well. If and when they got injured, it was her job to save their lives.

And she was extremely good at her job. Besides that there was little benefit to dwelling on the multitude of dangers surrounding them.

She spent a few moments checking out the inside of the tent, not that there was much to see. There were two collapsible camp beds in it, and Kate dropped her Bergen onto the remaining available one. There might not be any buildings here but at least there were beds. And solar showers, she remembered with satisfaction. She had not always been that lucky, and compared to some of the places she had been this was almost luxurious. She decided she could compromise on the added safety of a few good Hesco walls.

A regulation military sleeping bag lay neatly on top of the other bed, and Kate took a second to flick through the scuba diving magazine which had been left open by the side of it. Tough if you were into scuba diving in a place like this, she reflected. There was an open box of water bottles on the floor, and notebooks and maps piled high on an overturned crate which acted as a small table in between the two beds. Extra rations and several packets of pancake mix were tucked away in a corner, as well as a tough looking, battered guitar case.

Kate smiled a little at the sight of it, wondering about the woman who was in command of this platoon, who she would meet shortly. "The Boss", she mused, remembering the respectful way that Collins had referred to her throughout. She had to be good, Kate reflected, to get a post like this one. Cobel was in an extremely sensitive area of the country, and she had twelve men under her command... This was not the norm.

Unusually as well, there were no pictures in the tent, of loved ones, pets or any kind of life back at home. Nothing personal apart from the diving mag, guitar case and pancake mix.

Kate lay on top of her bed and closed her eyes, smiling a little. All in all this was pretty good, she reflected. It was really quite nice, and very unusual, that this Marines captain had managed to make such a good impression on her already, without even being around.

A very good start indeed.

The Boss, as Collins liked to refer to her, was lying on her stomach in a shallow ditch six miles to the East of Cobel. She was feeling a little bit cold, and hungry too, and she had spent the last twenty minutes or so visualising in her mind a mug of black coffee and a blueberry muffin. From time to time the muffin slowly morphed into a piece of vanilla cheesecake. Imagination was a wonderful thing. Tyler was happy going back and forth with that in her head. Doing what she had to do in order to stay awake, stay safe, and do her job.

Her eyes were trained on what appeared to be a completely deserted compound half a mile away. For hours now she had seen nothing move, heard nothing. It was tedious work. But despite the cold and the tiredness, she was alert, focused, and ready to spend another three hours in that ditch if it was what the mission required.

"Sitrep?" she murmured into her radio.

"Standby."

She recognised the voice of her commanding officer as he came on. Major Tim Cox may have been in an Ops tent in Bastion twenty miles away, but the Comms link was so good it felt like he was on the ground right next to her.

She had to wait a few minutes for him to give her the info she had asked for. While she waited she slowly scanned the area in front of her and to the sides, aware that her men were close by in the darkness, although they were so well concealed that she was unable to see them. They were the best. She felt confident knowing that she had their backup and that she was not alone in the night.

After what felt like an eternity Cox came back on the radio. He sounded pissed off, and rightly so.

"Your team is being stood down captain," he advised. "They're not coming."

Tyler exhaled slowly. All for nothing, she thought. She felt the tiniest bit of frustration, but she quickly got over it. She no longer got annoyed about these things now. It was not the first time they had received promising intelligence which then turned out to be useless, and it was all part of the job. This time, the leaders of a local Taliban group had been expected at the compound for a meeting. According to their initial information they were four hours late. Now Tyler understood why.

"Where did this new info come from, major?" she asked.

She trusted him of course, and she wanted to trust their source, whoever they were. But she would not risk moving herself and the men under her command until she was absolutely certain that it was safe to do so.

Cox reassured her quickly.

"The Intel guys intercepted a call from their original contact. It's all been verified. You can go home, captain, and watch yourself on the way back."

"Roger that," Tyler replied.

She stood up slowly, wincing at the pain in her back, and looked to her left. She smiled a little when she spotted the silent figures of her team emerging from the shadows. It was four of them, and they moved quickly and quietly toward her.

Lenster, Sneath, Andrews and Kelsey. Tall, fit, dressed in black from head to toe with cam cream covering their faces, necks and hands. They were a scary looking bunch, but to Tyler they were simply her friends.

"Endex," she announced simply. "Lenster, you take point, all right?"

"Yeah boss."

"Okay, let's go."

She took a position at the back behind Andrews and glanced up at the sky to confirm that the moon was still safely hidden behind a mass of clouds. Even though the Taliban would not be coming tonight, she could not afford to relax just yet. It was an easy walk back to base across a few fields and a couple of dirt tracks, but it was anything but safe.

Tyler rolled her shoulders a couple of times, her body warming up now that she was on the move, her back no longer aching. She was gazing far ahead, not focusing on anything in particular, her mind and senses on full alert. She used her peripheral vision and a sharp awareness of her surroundings to constantly monitor the area. When she sensed movement on her right, she immediately dropped to the ground.

"Down," she ordered quietly.

Immediately the marines melted into the field.

Tyler's heart rate had just spiked up significantly. She heard Lenster's voice whispering in her earpiece, confirming what she had only sensed.

"Got movement up ahead. One o'clock."

Tyler stared in that direction. For a little while nothing moved. Then she saw them.

Three figures, dressed in black, moving furtively through the trees on the far side of the field. Tyler had no idea how they could have failed to spot the soldiers crossing it, but it seemed that for now she and her team were still in the clear.

She narrowed her eyes at them as the three strangers stopped a little way away. She could hear them now.

Convinced that they had not been spotted, she raised her head a little to get a better look. They were carrying tools. They could have been farmers, but why would they be moving at night looking like they were hiding?

"Major?" she whispered over her radio.

The answer from Cox was immediate.

"Go ahead captain."

"We have eyes on three guys, real close."

"Taliban?"

Tyler winced in frustration.

"Not confirmed yet."

Kelsey cut in.

"One of them is carrying an AK, that's confirmed," he whispered.

From his position, slightly closer to the men than Tyler was, he could see at least one of them was armed. Then again, this was not unusual in itself. The men dropped a heavy bag on to the ground and squatted down next to it. Kelsey leaned forward as much as he dared and watched them through a pair of infrared binoculars. When he saw what they were taking out of the bag he flattened himself against the ground once more.

"IEDs," he hissed through his mic. "Bag's full of em."

"Permission to engage, major," Tyler said immediately.

"Wait out."

Her heart was hammering in her chest, and she concentrated on breathing calmly and remaining still. Up ahead the men had dropped their weapons on the ground and started digging.

"Weapons confirmed," Tyler told Cox over the radio.

How stupid were these guys, she wondered, almost shaking her head in disbelief. They were making every single mistake in the book. If her team were to engage them now, there was no way they would be able to respond. She got impatient as she waited for her green light.

"Sir," she murmured. "Now or never…"

"Understood, captain. You are cleared to engage. Take them alive if
you can."

"Roger," Tyler murmured, wasting no time with his last comment, a completely unnecessary reminder. She was not in the business of killing people for the fun of it, no matter who they were.

At this point there was not a lot of thinking to be done. The marines were already almost perfectly positioned around the three

Taliban fighters.

"Nice and slow," Tyler whispered over the team radio. "Let's get closer, then hard and fast."

It was a well-rehearsed manoeuvre, practised hundreds of times. Hard and fast meant the marines would act so quickly that their targets would be too stunned to react. They would use maximum speed and maximum force, and unleash hell onto their prey. The method was simple, tried and tested. It worked. Still, Tyler could feel the blood pounding in her head as she crawled forward, agonisingly slowly it seemed, but still completely unnoticed by the Taliban. It was the anticipation of battle she was used to, the huge rush of adrenaline that always preceded any action against the enemy.

When she was close enough to smell their cigarettes, she went still.

"Ready?" she murmured.

She got four radio clicks in reply.

Affirmative. Her guys were ready to pounce.

Tyler took a deep breath and steadied herself.

"On three," she said. "One, two..."

At the count of three the marines jumped up and rushed forward.

"GET DOWN! NOW! ON YOUR KNEES! COME ON, COME ON!"

The Taliban never stood a chance. By the time they realised what was happening the marines had them. Tyler aimed her weapon at one of the guys' face, seeing stunned disbelief in his eyes.

"Down," she ordered roughly.

Whether or not he could speak English, he had no problem understanding that command and wisely dropped to his knees.

Lenster's target decided to play dumb, but a well-aimed kick to the stomach soon got him down on the ground. The third guy tried to run but in his haste to get away only managed to collide with Kelsey, who easily knocked him down. When he looked up he found himself staring into the barrel of the big marine's rifle.

They were searched and cuffed quickly, and Tyler got back on the radio. Her hands were shaking a little. She tried to keep her voice steady, but adrenaline was literally making her feel out of breath.

"Sir, we're secure," she reported back to Cox.

"Casualties?"

"None."

"Well done captain. What have you got?"

Tyler glanced toward Andrews, who was holding the Taliban bag open for her.

"Three suspected Taliban, laying IEDs," she confirmed.

"Excellent."

She smiled at the excitement she could hear in Cox's voice.

"Good job, marines," he repeated. "The night wasn't a complete waste of time, now, was it?"

They were back inside Cobel less than an hour later, safe and sound, just as dawn was starting to break. Their prisoners were quickly whisked away to a nearby tent, to be flown to Bastion on the first available Chinook.

Tyler was the last one to enter the safety of the compound, and only then did she allow herself to drop her guard.

"Thanks, guys," she said as her team all regrouped around her, grinning and pleased with their work. "Good effort tonight, really good result. Well done."

"Wasn't that hard, boss," Kelsey commented with a shrug. "Those dudes obviously had no brains."

"Begging to get caught," Andrews agreed with a smirk.

Tyler smiled at them.

She knew they would have liked a good battle. For soldiers of their calibre, tonight's operation had been almost too easy. They trained to fight hard and they expected to be doing just that.

She knew better.

"No casualties is what matters," she reminded them. "Now make sure you get something to eat, and get some sleep, okay?"

Tyler was due a shower and some downtime herself before she went to bed, and she hurried back to her tent, stopping dead in her tracks when she spotted the other person asleep on the free bed.

She had forgotten all about the new medic, although she had been briefed on the fact that she would not be enjoying a tent of her own for much longer. Having spent all her life in the military so far, this was not a problem for her.

She glanced at the still form on the bed, unable to make out much of Kate, hidden as she was deep inside her sleeping bag. Her rifle was clean and within easy reach, Tyler noticed, and this was good, she thought approvingly.

Silently, she dropped her gear by the side of her own bed, reached for her wash kit, and chuckled to herself when a contented little snore sounded from somewhere deep inside the sleeping bag.

There was no need to wake Kate straight away, and so she walked out again silently, leaving her to enjoy some rest while she still could. There was no telling when things might get crazy around Cobel.

Chapter Two

Kate woke up with a start a little while later, immediately on the alert. She cast a quick glance toward the still empty bed next to her, blinking as she took in the dusty Bergen now propped up against it. The diving mag had been replaced by a well-worn helmet and a pair of Oakley sunglasses.

"Shit!" she muttered under her breath.

She had wanted to make a good first impression on the marines captain when she got back from patrol, and it looked like she had missed her. As it was, she had probably been snoring away.

"Bloody hell," she exclaimed.

She jumped up and fished in her rucksack for a clean t-shirt, pulled it on, quickly brushed her teeth using ice cold water from her bottle, and walked out into the early morning sunshine.

Squinting, she reached for her sunglasses, and aimed for the smell of breakfast that seemed to originate from a tent on the far right. In her experience, following the food trail was always a good idea in any military setting.

She slowed down a bit as she approached people, looking around her with interest. She did not recognise anyone from the night before. A few marines glanced her way and nodded; a few smiled at her and tossed some friendly hellos. Everybody was busy getting on with something, and the place was buzzing with activity.

As she looked around, she noticed a woman who stood in front of one of the tents, mug of coffee in hand, deep in conversation with a couple of the guys.

Kate stopped abruptly and did a quick double take, focusing her eyes on her.

The woman looked to be a little bit thinner than she was but just as tall, lean and strong looking. She was dressed like most of the men around her in desert boots and combat trousers, and she wore a tight sand-coloured t-shirt with the crest of the USMC on the front and a line underneath it that read: "If it bleeds, we can kill it." Typical Marines humour.

The captain's hair was cut short and looked a little messy, a darker shade of blond. She had a youthful and very energetic look about her which immediately made it a little difficult for Kate to take her eyes off her. She laughed out loud and said something that Kate did not catch, and the men around her all burst out laughing as well, before walking off in different directions.

Tyler spotted the medic at that moment, watching her from a distance, and she raised a hand up in greeting. She jogged her way over, looking light on her feet and comfortable as she greeted a few marines along the way, smiling and joking, looking for all the world like she owned the place and everything and everyone in it.

"Good morning," she said when she got near, smiling. "I'm Tyler."

No rank, no last name, just a very straight-forward and friendly greeting. She held out her hand to Kate, her clear grey eyes holding her gaze without the slightest trace of hesitation. The woman oozed that very special kind of understated confidence which some people would have called charismatic.

Kate opted for sexy as hell.

She shook the woman's hand and offered a smile of her own.

"I'm Kate. Sorry I missed you when you came back to the tent," she added quickly. "I don't normally oversleep like that."

Tyler just shrugged good-naturedly.

"No problem. You looked like you were enjoying your sleep, so I tried to be quiet. I'm ready for another coffee and a chat, how about you?"

"That would be great, thanks."

A few minutes later, and Tyler had a fresh pot on the go in one of the nearby tents. Kate sat down on a bench next to her and watched her, not bothering to hide her interest.

Up close and personal the woman looked young, she noticed. Yet the relaxed and confident way she addressed the older marines around her, men who were lower in rank but who looked way harder and tougher than she did, hinted at combat experience of the highest calibre. Kate was reminded that people tended to grow up fast in the military. And talent also tended to be spotted quickly and rewarded accordingly.

Tyler's face was lightly tanned, her features sharp and precise. She looked like an athlete, and everything about her screamed military excellence. For all that, she still had a little bit of cam cream stuck to the underside of her jaw. It looked almost like chocolate ice cream, and Kate had a sudden crazy urge to lean forward and rub it off with her finger.

Feeling herself start to blush, she cleared her throat and mentally shook herself.

"So, busy night?" she enquired.

"Yes. Productive night," Tyler replied with a quick smile and a friendly glance toward her. "We waited for a bunch of Taliban who never showed up, but then we bumped into another group of them placing IEDs into the ground. Got three prisoners."

She poured thick black coffee into a tin mug and hesitated.

"I'm afraid we're out of milk and sugar."

"Black is great, thank you," Kate replied.

"Are you hungry?"

Kate's stomach rumbled at the thought of food.

"I'll take that as a yes," Tyler commented, smiling. "Good."

"I'm starving actually... I think the last meal I had was in Kandahar. Feels like years ago."

"What did you have?"

"I went to the steak house."

Tyler licked her lips and stopped moving, her eyes on Kate and her gaze intense.

"I've been there a couple of times," she said. "It's the one next to the hospital, right?"

"That's right."

"So what did you have?"

"Mexican burger. Double cheddar, chilli sauce, guacamole. Side order of fries with mayo. And a Coke." Kate did her best not to grin, but her chocolate brown eyes were sparkling with amusement. "It was ok," she said modestly.

Tyler stared at her in silence for a second, and then she burst out laughing.

"Oh, are you kidding me?" she exclaimed. "You've just described my dream meal. What I wouldn't give for one of those Kandahar feasts right now!"

Kate chuckled quietly.

"Sorry. You did ask…"

"I certainly did," Tyler admitted, still laughing. "And I'm glad you enjoyed it. But it's ration packs only out here I'm afraid."

"Oh, come on, really? This is an American outpost, right? Where are the Starbucks and the McDonalds?"

Tyler shook her head, amused at the gentle teasing.

She squatted next to a wooden crate and started rummaging inside.

"I guess they reserve that for you Brits at glitzy Kandahar. It's back to basics here."

"Bugger."

"You got that right. I think. You do speak English, right?"

"I'll try my best not to confuse you too much with my lingo, captain."

"Awesome, dude," Tyler said in an exaggerated drawl.

Her voice was warm, husky, and it was obvious that she was

enjoying the easy banter between them. Kate relaxed. Smiling, she took a sip of her coffee.

"Nice," she said. "So you like pancakes?"

"Yep. I see you spotted my secret stash, right? I think it's good for morale sometimes."

"I would imagine you need it often in this sort of place," Kate commented.

"Oh, I don't know about that... I guess the marines are pretty good at focusing on the positive stuff and ignoring all the rest. "

Tyler passed the crate over to Kate and she sat on the ground across from her. She bit into a Powerbar and took a sip of her coffee. She chewed in silence for a few seconds, thinking about what Kate had just said.

She did not have a lot of time to think about her surroundings or living conditions very often. She was an officer, and her job pretty much demanded and absorbed every single drop of energy she had to give out here on the frontline. It was relentless, and in truth she relished the single-mindedness of that lifestyle. No time to think about herself or her personal needs, no time to be alone with any unwanted thoughts, just the punishing schedule of planning patrols, looking after her men, and making sure that they all stayed alive. Just the way she wanted it.

She stole a few glances at Kate as the medic opted for a packet of instant porridge, smiling a little at the look of utter concentration on her face as she got her meal ready. When Kate looked up and caught her staring, captivating brown eyes locking onto her own and holding her gaze, it was Tyler's turn to find it quite difficult to look away. The medic was good looking, to say the least, and it was not lost on Tyler that she had been doing a fair amount of staring herself. Kate sat back and licked her spoon clean, a gesture which again made Tyler want to laugh.

"Porridge, uh," she said. "Very healthy of you, doc."

"Yes. My kind of comfort food," Kate explained. "Reminds me of home."

"And where is that?"

"I'm from Yorkshire."

"I've never been to England," Tyler reflected. "And the past few years I've spent more time in Iraq and Afghanistan than I have at home."

"Where are you from originally?"

"I grew up just outside of San Francisco."

Kate's eyes sparkled.

"That's nice," she said. "I've been there. Been to Alcatraz."

"Yeah." Tyler laughed. "It's an amazing place to visit, as long as you get to go home at the end of the day."

She was glad to find that the new medic was so friendly and easy going. Life at Cobel was not easy, to say the least, and a sense of humour was essential. She suspected that Kate would settle down quickly and get on well with all the guys.

"So, what do you miss most about home?" she asked.

Kate gave her a knowing smile, as if the answer was obvious.

"Power showers," she said without hesitation. "Always will be. Showers, shampoo, conditioner, the lot."

She smiled again and her entire face lit up, and Tyler laughed with her, still finding it quite difficult not to stare. When she had first spotted Kate watching her from across camp, she had not thought much about her beyond the fact that the new medic looked very fit, and like she could handle spending several hours out on patrol with the platoon. Good stuff. But now Tyler was finding herself unusually attracted to her quick smile, her deep, intelligent brown eyes, and the amusing way that Kate seemed so interested in watching her and not bothered if it showed. She appeared confident, and relaxed. The British accent was a nice touch too.

Tyler was captivated.

"What else do you miss?" she asked.

"Clean clothes. A proper bed. The Great British Bake off."

"The what?"

"Cookery show. Baking competition."

"Right."

"About as far from what I do in life as you can get. Great escapism. I can sit through hours of the stuff."

Tyler chuckled.

"Sure sounds good to me," she agreed.

She ran her fingers through her short hair, looking happy as she took another sip of her coffee.

"So what about you?" Kate asked, watching her with the same undisguised curiosity. "What do you miss most about home?"

"All of the above," Tyler replied. "Minus your baking thing, but it sounds like something I could get into."

"What else?" Kate insisted, eager to hear something personal about the young captain.

"I miss the sea," Tyler answered straight away. "And being able to walk on the beach without having to worry that there are mines in the sand."

Kate saw grief flicker in her eyes before Tyler glanced away quickly, and she kicked herself for being so pushy.

When she looked at Kate again Tyler's face was intense, and the emotion linked to the memory of the friends she had lost to IEDs had added an intense sparkle to her already bright eyes. She looked a little bit older too. She gave the medic a long look, her expression now serious and completely impossible to read.

"So what is your brief here?" she asked. "The boss said you want to focus on seeing the women in the villages?"

"That's right."

"Like a one-woman female engagement team?"

Kate gave a soft laugh.

"Yes, pretty much. Only I want to focus more on the medical side of things."

"Of course." Tyler nodded approvingly. "Yeah, we can do that."

She seemed to relax again all of a sudden, and she leaned forward a little, inviting further questions.

"Have you met or spoken to a lot of the local women?" Kate enquired, keen to hear her side of things.

"A few. Not many."

"Is it hard to get access to them?"

"It can be," Tyler nodded. "And they're all pretty shy at first. We tell them that there are Afghan women out there in the army, in the police, women like them. But this area is so remote. It's like they're ten years behind, if not more."

"It would be nice if we could get some of these Afghan role models to come out here to visit," Kate mused.

Tyler flashed her an approving smile.

"I agree. Might be a few years off in the making still... But the next generation? I really hope so."

"So the local people are friendly then. Right?"

"I think they're on side for the most part. All they want is to be happy and get on with their lives. But we won't always be here to protect them against the Taliban and they are terrified of what will happen then. Their own children get blown up by IEDs too, you know."

"I know," Kate said gently.

Tyler sounded tired and frustrated all of a sudden, and Kate knew she had been up all night working. Keen to wrap things up and let the woman get some well-deserved rest, she started to tidy up for the both of them.

"I understand you have two other medics on site?" she asked as she worked.

"Yes, I'll get Collins to introduce you to the guys. They're attached to 3 Platoon."

"Cool. And I'm happy to be with you," Kate said.

She meant it, and it showed. Tyler smiled at her, and the little glint of sadness in her eyes that Kate had been able to spot from time to time disappeared instantly.

"Thanks. It's good to have you with us too," she said softly.

She lingered for a couple of seconds, and as she gazed into the British medic's intense brown eyes again, she was surprised to realise how happy she felt.

Chapter Three

After that first day Kate wasted no time getting into the swing of things. Ben Collins introduced her to the other medics, Rich Fallon and Matt Hibbert, both from New York City. Rich was a reserve officer and a paramedic at home. Matt was an ex-Navy guy and had been a specialist medic for the past five years. She fell easily into their routine, and found that they made a good team. The guys were laid back and friendly, yet extremely knowledgeable and professional. It suited Kate's own style.

Whenever a patrol went out a medic always accompanied them, and the other two handled backup at the FOB. Kate tried to be a part of Tyler's missions as much as she could, and she was grateful that the captain built time in her patrols for visits to the friendliest compounds in the area.

Kate felt that she was allowed to do her job properly, and that her mission was recognised and backed up as it should. For that reason alone she was enjoying her time at Cobel, and she owed it to Tyler.

On a late afternoon three weeks later, Kate joined her at the back of the compound, where the guys had built a makeshift gym. Tyler was on her own. She was lying on a bench on her stomach, holding light weights in her hands, her movements mimicking a front crawl action.

"Missing a swimming pool, uh?" Kate called out.

Tyler turned her head a little, spotted her, and dropped the weights on the dusty ground.

"Yeah. I told command we should build one and invite the Taliban over for a swim meet."

"Oh, really, how did that go?"

Tyler stood up and grinned.

"They said no. Go figure."

She was wearing her standard combat trousers, desert boots, and a simple black Nike sports bra. Kate spotted the tattoo just above her hip bone and immediately stepped forward for a closer look. She recognised the famous M, and reached out to softly trace the outline of it with a finger. Tyler's stomach muscles twitched involuntarily, and Kate looked at her questioningly.

The captain stood watching her with a serious expression on her face, and her eyes were a little bit darker than usual. Kate thought she recognised that look. It was a warning all right. She dropped her hand.

"Ironman," she said admiringly. "You've done one?"

"I did Ironman Arizona last year with a bunch of the guys, and the year before we did Kona," Tyler replied. "You?"

"Jesus, no," Kate exclaimed, laughing and taking a step back as if the simple fact of talking about it might be a dangerous thing.

"Well, you recognised the tattoo, you must be interested. Are you looking to do one?"

Kate shook her head.

"You couldn't pay me enough," she said with feeling. "But my ex-girlfriend did one in Nottingham a few years ago. Looked like torture to me, but she says she enjoyed it."

Tyler nodded curtly.

"Right," she said.

She felt a little tense all of a sudden. She was not sure of the rules in the British Army, but she had learnt to keep her private life private. She walked toward the exercise bar wedged in between two branches of a small tree, and gestured for Kate to come join her.

"Have you warmed up yet?" she asked.

Kate did not reply straight away, distracted by the sight of Tyler as she stood sipping from a bottle, her face angled toward the sun and her eyes closed. A little droplet of sweat was licking its way down the side of her neck as she drank, and for a second Kate became lost in thoughts. It only lasted a second though, because Tyler turned back to her with an eyebrow raised.

Kate grinned at her.

"No need, I'm ready to go," she said, and she jumped up and got a good grip on the exercise bar.

Smiling, Tyler took a couple of steps back to observe. The medic looked good up there, she thought. It was obvious that she knew what she was doing.

Kate executed a few perfect pull ups, looking effortless and very slick in her technique.

"Looking good, doc," Tyler commented.

"Haven't even started yet!"

"Is that right?" Tyler said with a chuckle.

She saw the bar slip off the branch just as Kate finished her tenth pull up, and she watched in dismay as the woman went flying off backwards.

"Kate!"

Tyler rushed forward but she was too late to break her fall. Kate landed on her back with a lot of force, her head slamming against one side of the metal bench as she hit the deck hard. It literally knocked the breath out of her, and for a moment she was too stunned to even move or say anything.

Tyler immediately knelt by her side and rested a firm hand on her shoulder.

"Hey. Kate? Are you all right?" she asked urgently.

Kate breathed out slowly. She could see black spots dancing in front of her eyes, and she was confused about the loud buzzing sound inside her head.

"Doc. Talk to me," Tyler insisted.

Finally, her voice broke through Kate's consciousness.

"Yeah... Just a sec..." she murmured.

Her stomach rolled, and she squeezed her eyes shut. If she did not concentrate she would probably be sick, and if there was one person she did not want to watch her throw up it was Tyler, who seemed like the most accomplished and professional officer in camp, and certainly would have much better control of herself. Kate kept her eyes closed and she tried to keep on breathing evenly.

Meanwhile Tyler gently ran her fingers behind her neck and along her shoulders.

"Does this hurt at all?" she asked.

"No... Just tight..."

"Okay, good. Can you sit up?"

Kate hoped that she would be able to. She nodded and raised herself up on one elbow, and Tyler quickly slipped an arm around her shoulders to support her.

"Thanks," Kate murmured. "Sorry about this."

"Not your fault, Kate. Tell me if any of this hurts," Tyler said quietly.

She knelt behind Kate and again ran her fingers delicately along the back of her head, all the while watching her carefully.

"I'm all right, Tyler..."

"Yes. Just making sure. Lean back against me."

Kate allowed herself to do that for just a second. It felt good. She closed her eyes again and exhaled slowly, and she might have got lost in the feeling if Tyler's feather light touch on the back of her head had not revealed another really painful spot.

Kate's eyes flew open all of a sudden and she jerked forward out of the comfortable position.

"Don't touch it," she exclaimed, gritting her teeth against the pain.

"Sorry," Tyler apologised immediately.

She dropped her hand and Kate sat up a little straighter. She was feeling nauseous and very dizzy, although she did not want to admit it. Another thing that she was not ready to admit to herself was how good Tyler's careful touch on the back of her neck had felt, and how nice it had been to relax against her body.

Instead she tried to pretend that it was nothing and that she was completely recovered. She was a medic after all, and not supposed to be the one rolling around on the ground feeling sorry for herself.

"I'm okay," she said automatically. "Just a little winded."

She smiled, but all colour had left her face, and Tyler was no fool.

"You don't look so good Kate," she said gently. "Think you should
lie down for a bit maybe?"

"No. I'm fine. No need for drama."

Kate got to her feet quickly, before Tyler had a chance to help. Instantly light-headed, she swayed. Heavy, thick strands of darkness wrapped around her head and threatened to pull her down with them. There was no coming back from this one, and Tyler managed to catch her just as she fainted.

When Kate came to she found Ben Collins' face was obscuring most of her field of vision. The huge marine grinned as she opened her eyes, and she knew then that some kind of heartless ribbing was on the cards.

She squeezed her eyes shut again.

"Go away," she muttered.

"Hey doc, what's going on?" he chuckled. "Trying to get yourself shipped off home ahead of time, uh?"

"Kate, you awake?"

Her eyes snapped open again when she heard Matt's voice. Collins was walking away, laughing to himself.

"How are you doing?" her American colleague asked.

His eyes were bright and searching as they focused on her face.

"Fine," she said quickly.

"Uh uh."

He wrapped his fingers around her wrist and rested a cool hand on her forehead. Feeling hugely embarrassed, Kate brushed his hand away.

"I'm okay. Please don't fuss, Matt."

"Ah, a typical doctor answer," he remarked with a grin. "Are you bullshitting me or what?"

Kate looked around her and recognised the infirmary.

"What am I doing here?" she protested. "I'm not kidding, I'm fine."

"Yes, but you were out for a good ten minutes regardless," Matt replied, sounding amused. "Plenty of time for us to worry."

"Us?"

"Well. The captain was a bit concerned. Although Collins told her you Brits are all pretty hard-headed and that you'd probably bounce back in no time."

Kate smirked.

"Bet he did."

Her eyes searched the room, and she felt instant disappointment when she realised that the officer they were talking about was not present.

"Where is Tyler?" she asked, trying for casual but not quite managing it.

Matt narrowed his eyes at her, looking way too interested in her reaction.

"She had to rush off. Got called out on a shout. Why?"

Kate's pulse immediately quickened.

"What kind of a shout?" she asked, ignoring his question.

"A patrol got ambushed on the other side of the river. They needed additional firepower, so she's gone out with the guys of 2 Platoon."

Kate's blood started to pound at the news. She sat up suddenly, swinging her legs over the side of the bed.

"Hey, where do you think you're going?" Matt exclaimed.

He looked just about ready to try to stop her, and she silenced him with a warning look before he could even try.

"Hey, thanks for checking me out. But I'm going to see if I can make myself useful at the Ops tent."

In the end there was not much else for Kate to do but sit around and wait, which, considering her line of work, was in fact pretty good news. And the platoon did not make it back to base until well into the night, by which time she was dozing inside her sleeping bag. She awoke just after midnight at the sound of suspicious rustling inside the tent, and immediately reached for her weapon. Jumping off the bed and adopting a defensive position, she gasped a little when she saw who she was aiming her gun at.

"Hey, doc."

Tyler was eyeing her calmly, looking like she did not really mind having a nine millimetre pointed straight at her head. Kate lowered her hand, very carefully.

"Tyler," she said, and she sounded slightly out of breath.

"Yep, only me."

"Sorry. Oh, God, you nearly gave me a heart attack..."

"Just please don't shoot me before I've had a chance to shower, okay?" Tyler muttered, shaking her head in pretend annoyance.

Kate could see her eyes were sparkling with amusement. Her hair was stiff with dirt and she looked exhausted, and yet in Kate's opinion she still managed to look gorgeous. Her gaze grew gentle as she watched her take off her body armour and gloves. It was happening, she could not help it.

"Hey," she said softly. "I'm glad you're back. Sorry it looked like I wasn't."

"No worries, Kate. Nothing wrong with being alert and ready. And yes, I'm glad we're back too. Wasn't an easy job. Anyway, how is your head?"

"All good. I just…"

"Stood up too quickly, I know," Tyler interrupted, laughing. "Only asking, not getting dramatic about it, don't worry."

Kate climbed back inside her sleeping bag and sat cross-legged on her bed.

"Yeah, well. Sorry. I admit I'm not a very good patient."

Tyler gave her a quick glance.

"Nah, you're all right," she said quietly.

Her tone was a little wistful, and Kate raised a questioning eyebrow. Tyler saw it and she smiled, almost shyly.

"I'm glad you're okay," she said simply. "You came down pretty hard, I was worried. And then I couldn't wait to make sure you were fine, so…"

"Thanks. But I was a lot safer inside here at the infirmary with Matt than you were out there on patrol."

Tyler shrugged a little.

"Are you not eating this?" Kate asked as she dropped her MRE, meal ready to eat, on the table.

"No. I'm not really hungry. I need a shower first I think, and to chill out for a bit."

"Was it bad out there today?" Kate enquired softly.

Tyler's expression became serious as she replayed the day's events in her head. Fighting, blood, fear. Soldiers getting hurt. She felt agitated and anxious.

"We did good work, on the whole," she reflected. "The patrol out there had lost two guys by the time we managed to reach them. But after we got stuck in, nobody else died. I guess that's a result."

She looked tired, Kate noticed, and a little angry too, which was unusual.

"Are you okay, really?" she asked.

Tyler took a deep breath and stood up again.

"Yeah," she said firmly. "Sorry. Sometimes I just get a bit fed up."

"How do you mean?"

"Sometimes I can't really understand what we're doing here. Doesn't seem to make a blind bit of difference..."

She caught herself before she said any more. No whinging, she reminded herself. It was one of her personal rules. No matter how bad things got, she focused on the good, and simply got on with it. She did not question the policy, the rules, the mission or the politics. It had been her choice to join up. She had become expert at using it all to keep her mind off the things she did not want to remember. It worked for her.

She noticed that Kate was observing her with a concerned look in her eyes, and she smiled at her and touched her arm briefly.

"Don't worry doc. Just need a shower and some sleep, that's all."

Kate reached under her bed and retrieved a small bottle of shampoo she pressed into Tyler's hand.

"Here, take this. A present for you, to make you feel better," she said with a smile.

Tyler's eyes sparkled.

"Body Shop?" she exclaimed. "Cool! Where did you get that?"

"My friend Marion sent me some. She hates being stuck in the field almost as much as I do," Kate replied, laughing.

"That's nice of her. She's your friend? In the army?"

"Yes, she's a medic as well. We trained together back in the UK."

Tyler nodded a little and remained rooted to the spot. She was silent.

"Just so you know, she's not my girlfriend," Kate added, volunteering the information because she suspected Tyler would never have the nerve to ask her such a personal question.

Someone had to make the first move in these situations and she did not mind taking the lead. She moved closer to her, her voice barely a whisper now.

"What about you?"

Tyler frowned a little, her eyes roaming over Kate's face as if she had not understood the question.

"Me what?"

"Are you single?"

"Yeah."

"Well, that's good to know. But you like women, right?"

Tyler tensed and instinctively threw a worried look toward the flimsy canvas door.

"No one here but us," Kate reassured her. "So. Tell me?"

Tyler sighed. Razor sharp and straight to the point as usual. She had to admit that she really liked that about Kate.

"Yes, I do like women," she said slowly. "But you knew that already."

"I was hoping," Kate said, and she laughed when she saw the funny look that Tyler gave her. "I mean, it is nice to be amongst friends," she explained. "Know what I mean?"

"Yeah, I know," Tyler replied, just standing there, facing her. "It's nice."

She looked a little bit thoughtful, and a little bit distant as she said that, and far from convinced. Kate narrowed her eyes at her and got even closer.

"So how come you don't have a girlfriend?" she murmured.

Tyler took a little step back.

"My lifestyle isn't very conducive to relationships," she said simply.

She could not help but grin when Kate took a very obvious, and very deliberate step toward her.

"Ah, come on captain," she insisted, "it's me you're talking to. No bullshit."

She was smiling, and teasing, and careful not to push too hard, and yet there was no doubt that the interest in her eyes was genuine, and her smile went straight through Tyler's heart. She could do nothing but stare. This woman did care, she suddenly realised. She really wanted to know. To know her.

Suddenly she felt her chest constrict a little.

"That's just the way it is," she said softly, as if to herself.

She gave Kate a little squeeze on the shoulder as she walked past.

She needed to be alone.

"Thanks for the shampoo, doc."

Chapter Four

A few days later on what happened to be her birthday, Kate was out with the troop on another so called routine patrol. It all felt like second nature to her by then, yet she was far from complacent.

Earlier on that morning she had given everyone at Cobel a refresher lecture on haemorrhage management. Collins had volunteered to be her victim, and she had calmly detailed the injuries an IED was likely to cause someone, using a red marker pen to circle each spot on his body. People paid attention. And although most would have been taught this before, they all made sure that they could see clearly when she demonstrated how to tie on a tourniquet, and how to pack a wound.

Kate remembered how Tyler had stood at the front, looking focused, strong and confident. It was hard to believe that someone as capable and switched on as she was might become a victim. Yet Kate knew that as soon as they stepped out of the compound they were all vulnerable. And there was no such thing as a routine patrol. As Collins had said on her first day, there were no guarantees.

And on that particular day, improvements were definitely needed.

At the very exact time that she was born, thirty-five years earlier, Kate found herself under heavy fire, trying to hide inside a ditch filled with freezing water.

The next thing she knew, Tyler landed on top of her feet first. One of her boots connected with Kate's face, hard enough to knock her off balance. Happy birthday.

Kate got pushed hard against the side of the ditch, her legs buckling under her in the thick mud underneath. Tyler caught her just as she was about to go under.

"Shit! You okay?" she exclaimed over the noise of battle.

At the same time she readjusted Kate's helmet, and steadied her with a firm hand.

Disoriented, Kate nevertheless caught the flash of concern in the young captain's eyes, and she gave a quick nod. She did not need Tyler worrying about her in the middle of a firefight and losing concentration.

"I'm okay," she said quickly. "Don't worry."

She did not have time to say much more. Rounds were flying, and Tyler quickly pulled her down with her, squatting lower inside the ditch.

The platoon were pinned down inside a compound about two miles from base. They had got there okay in the morning, spoken to the locals, and Kate had managed to see a few villagers in need of medical attention, including a pregnant woman.

There had been a bunch of kids next door, and one of the little girls, who could not have been more than four or five years old, took a particular interest in Tyler. She was shy at first, but she could not take her eyes off the young officer. Once Tyler had removed her helmet and smiled at her from a distance, the little girl ran over and gazed expectantly up at her. When the captain sat on the ground next to her, the child climbed onto her lap as if they were old friends and stuck her thumb in her mouth, holding fast onto Tyler's hand and leaning against her chest with a sleepy look in her eyes. Tyler took it all in her stride, taking her time and enjoying the moment.

It had been a really nice surprise for Kate to see how quickly Tyler engaged with the kids in the compounds, and how well they responded to her. It was a side of her that she wished she could find out more about. She was hoping that one day perhaps they could meet again in what laughingly called "the real world." Where no one would be trying to kill them.

When she realised that they were leaving, and after Tyler had made the huge mistake of sharing some of her candy supplies with her, the little girl burst into tears, and she ran after them and screamed and held onto Tyler's leg until the woman finally picked her up and hugged her tight.

"Come on, little one," she said easily. "You're too young to go out on patrol with me. Okay?"

The child stopped crying immediately, and stared at her with huge brown eyes which reminded her a little of Kate's. Tyler smiled and gently handed her back to one of the women. She felt reluctant to leave, but she had learned long ago that it never paid to get too attached.

"Tell them to keep her in, yes?" she asked the interpreter. "She can't be running after us when we don't know what's out there."

She turned around without another look at the child, and the marines walked out of the compound in single file. Everybody was in good spirits, but as they prepared to exit the village it seemed to empty.

As if by magic, all of a sudden everybody was indoors, leaving the soldiers in no doubt as to what was about to come. Tyler got on the radio to base to say that the "atmospherics", a marines term to describe the feel of a situation, had gone bad, and nervous anticipation rippled through the platoon.

Collins got the good news first when a round missed his head by a few inches, and he dived to the ground yelling.

"Contact! Contact!" he screamed, and his voice echoed through the team radios.

All of a sudden the situation worsened, and with shouts of "RPG, incoming!", several marines were scrambling for safety. Kate jumped out of the way into the first pocket of safety she could see, a ditch that was running underneath one of the village walls. And five seconds later Tyler threw herself in after her.

Still holding on to Kate's arm tightly, she crawled out of the ditch until they were just on the other side of the wall.

"Stay close to me, okay?" she instructed, and as Kate nodded silently, she stopped moving and got on the radio.

"Talk to me guys," she said. "Collins. Everybody okay?"

Her voice was so calm and matter of fact she might as well have been discussing the local weather with a bunch of friends.

Everybody was fine. Reports of shots being fired and their estimated location were exchanged. Satisfied that everyone on her team was safe, Tyler turned to look at Kate again. Her eye was bleeding a little and she was pale. Tyler rested a gloved hand on her shoulder.

"Hey, doc?" she said softly.

Kate met her gaze, looking slightly harried.

"Hang in there, okay?" Tyler told her with a smile. "We're going to get out of this one as quickly as we can."

Kate nodded, hating herself for appearing so weak, and yet right there and then she really was feeling scared and out of her depth. Tyler turned her attention back to the fight as an explosion sounded behind them, uncomfortably close. The ground shook and Kate flinched, feeling the energy from the impact all the way through to the centre of her chest. Unconsciously she pressed herself harder against Tyler.

She had been shot at before, but never like this, never with such intent, from such close distance.

This was bad.

"Collins, send our grid reference to base, tell them we need air support," Tyler said over the radio. "Guys, it's coming from that wood on the left, see it?"

"Yeah, we're hammering it," came the immediate response.

"How come they're still firing then?" Tyler exclaimed sharply, and she set her sights on the trees in the distance.

She could just make out a figure behind a cluster of walls slightly to the right of the wood. The figure darted in and out, and it looked like the guy was on a mobile phone.

"They're dicking us, and they are not shy about it," she announced, and again her voice was calm, but Kate was lying very close to her and she could feel the tension radiating from her body.

"Are we getting any I-Comm?"

I-Comm, or Intercepted Communications, was the name for Taliban radio chatter. The marines always tried to tap in to it, and they had trained interpreters relaying every single word of the current conversation back to them.

"Yeah, they're saying they got us pinned down and not to let us leave," Collins responded.

He too sounded very calm, almost bored, although Kate knew he would be anything but.

"Apache will be three minutes boss," he confirmed.

"Good," Tyler acknowledged. Then she gave Kate a quick glance and muttered: "See how they like having a Hellfire dropped on their heads, right?"

She settled more comfortably into position and zeroed in on the figure in the dish dash. The guy was getting bolder, spending more time in the open, getting a good look at their positions.

Tyler's thoughts drifted back to the little girl from the compound and her heart tightened. She wished she could have gone back and made sure that she was safe. But she had a job to do, and sticking her nose into the locals' business was not a part of it. So as always she focused on the business side of things, and tuned out every other thought, every feeling and emotion. She dropped the man into her sights. Male adult. Mobile phone. Unmistakable. Her index finger dropped on to the trigger and she breathed deeply.

While Tyler's attention was focused on the Taliban fighter, Kate was looking at her. Her heart was pounding, her head hurt and she was covered in dirt, wet and cold from the ditch. She was scared. She did not want to be there... Or did she? She realised that given the choice, she probably would not have wanted to be anywhere else.

She was more than a little surprised by her reaction to Tyler, and she was not entirely sure how she felt about it, but there was no denying the attraction.

As she observed her now, Kate felt exhausted, terrified and excited all at the same time. She remembered how happy and relaxed Tyler had looked earlier on when she had been playing with the children from the compound. But now all of this was long gone, and Tyler looked different, dangerous, almost frightening even to Kate. This was a professional soldier about to kill another human being that Kate was looking at now, and she shivered and glanced away quickly as Tyler bit her lower lip in concentration and prepared to shoot.

Her index finger tightened on the trigger. She exhaled slowly, held her breath, and fired a couple of rounds. She watched her target fall as he took a direct hit through the forehead. Through her sights she saw his skull explode in grim, sharp detail. That she would kill him was never in doubt. The fact that she would feel nothing when her bullets hit was also a given. She felt no emotion whatsoever, apart from satisfaction at having stopped him.

Someone's voice came on the radio.

"Good shootin' boss."

Tyler blew air out loudly, and looked away from her sights to glance at Kate and reassure herself that she was still there. Her eyes were dark, her expression unreadable, and soon the Apache was right on top of them.

The pilot's voice came on the net.

"Monster call sign, Monster call sign, one Hellfire, into the wood. Time on target, five seconds."

There were several excited shouts from the troops as the helicopter hit the wood with one of the most powerful missiles they carried, vaporising whoever had been trying to kill the marines.

Quiet followed intense activity, and Kate took a deep breath, realising for the first time that blood was running into her right eye and that her legs were shaking.

She sat up slowly.

"Let me have a look," Tyler said immediately.

"There's no need."

"Come on, Kate, let me see," Tyler insisted, and the gentleness in her voice was irresistible.

Kate sat up straighter and allowed her to get closer. She grew a little still as Tyler knelt in front of her and rested a finger under her chin, lifting her head gently. Kate found herself looking deep into her eyes, and when Tyler rested her other hand on the back of her neck, her heart started to beat a little faster.

"Don't worry, I'm fine," she repeated firmly.

"I gave you a black eye, I'm sorry," Tyler said, her eyes serious as she examined the wound. "And you're bleeding."

"I'll get it sorted when we get home."

"Home?" Tyler snorted. "Must have hit you harder than I thought if you call it that. Anyway, good tactical move, jumping into that ditch."

She kept on smiling softly at Kate, as if waiting to see what the other woman would say.

"Yeah, all I can tell you is next time find your own ditch," Kate shot back with fake indignation.

She had to say something funny, otherwise she was afraid that her expression would betray her thoughts. As it was she was not sure that it was enough to completely hide what was going through her head. And she was finding it difficult to remain still with Tyler sitting so close to her.

The captain chuckled and gave a light little shrug.

"Maybe I enjoy your company doc," she said softly.

There was some noise behind them, and they both turned to look.

"Fucking good job boss!" Collins' voice called out.

Tyler winked playfully at Kate, who looked back over her

shoulder.

"What, decking the medic?" she said, and she laughed quietly when he took one look at Kate and froze.

"Hell," he said solemnly. "You guys had a fight?"

"Oh, come on, it's not that bad," Kate protested. "I know it's not that bad."

Collins grinned, enjoying letting off a little bit of steam with them. He nodded at Tyler, and stepped forward to give Kate a hand up.

"I say let's get out of here, hey boss?" he smiled. "Taliban nil, USA 110."

Kate was smiling when she noticed that Tyler was staring past Collins, toward the compound, the expression on her face intense once more. Before Kate could ask her what was wrong she stood up quickly, and walked off without another word.

"What... What's going on?" Kate exclaimed, puzzled.

Collins stood close to her, very alert, listening hard to the net. Then he swore under his breath.

"Shit. It sounds like some of the locals got hit."

Kate started jogging after him. She could see a small crowd gathering up ahead, all local men, about ten of them. She glanced at Collins, recognising the potential for trouble. But he just gave her a small nod and carried on.

When Kate got closer she spotted a young boy of about sixteen lying on the ground in the middle, covered in blood. She could see that he was conscious. Forgetting her own safety, Kate pushed through the group of men so she could get to him. Collins was right behind her. He knew enough Pashto to understand that the locals were angry at the Taliban, not the Americans. So he was happy to let Kate go about her business. He nodded several times as one of the older men asked if Kate could help.

"Is that boy going to be okay, doc?" he asked her. "Can you help?"

"Yes… And yes I can."

Kate worked quickly, checking the boy's body for any obvious and more serious wounds, finding nothing that worried her too much. He had a big gash in his right arm, probably the result of some flying shrapnel, and it was bleeding a fair bit. But it was definitely not life threatening. Kate told Collins that, and he relayed that information to the men. One of them clasped his shoulder, smiling. Collins smiled back, and asked if anybody else was in need of medical attention. All the while he was scanning the area, checking that every marine in the troop were doing what they were supposed to do. He doubted very much that any Taliban fighters would have stuck around after the attack, but he would not take any chances.

Then he suddenly realised that he had lost sight of Tyler, and he got onto her frequency immediately.

"Boss?" he asked.

"Be there in a minute," Tyler answered, and she sounded keyed up to the extreme.

Collins frowned, and he turned back to Kate.

"Nearly done there, Kate?" he asked.

"Yes, he'll be fine now," she answered.

She had cleaned the wound thoroughly, stitched him up, and wrapped his arm up in a thick bandage. All in record time. The boy was grinning a little, obviously enjoying all the attention.

Kate ruffled his hair and stood up.

"Where's Tyler?" she asked, tension returning as she scanned the males faces around them, looking for her friend who seemed to have disappeared.

Collins looked toward the far side of the compound, and nodded at one of his men as he started walking.

"Lenster, you're with me. Kate?"

"Yes, I'm coming."

Kate was worried now, and Collins' tense demeanour did nothing to reassure her. It was very unlike Tyler to go off on her own like that. Her fingers tingled and a wave of apprehension and adrenaline shot through her. She could hear crying and loud women voices coming from a little way away. She swore under her breath.

This did not sound good at all.

"Boss?" Collins asked again on the radio.

They got nothing but static this time, and Collins picked up the pace. He was about to call for more backup when Kate grabbed his arm and stopped him.

"There she is," she said, pointing to their left.

A group of women were huddled together in a corner of the compound. A few of them were crying loudly, holding on to each other and rocking. Kate's heart jumped in her chest when she spotted Tyler, kneeling on the ground in the middle of them. For a crazy second she thought that she might be hurt, and she found it hard to breathe. Then she realised that she was holding a small child in her arms, and as they got closer she recognised the little girl from before, the one who had sat on Tyler's lap and dozed in her arms. She did not need to ask to know that she was dead.

Collins exhaled sharply and stopped dead in his tracks.

"Ah, shit, they got a kid," he murmured under his breath. "Fucking bastards."

"What do we do now?" Kate asked tightly.

She was not looking at him. Her eyes were on Tyler.

"You go on," he told her. "But we have to leave soon. Is that clear, doc? Don't get caught up in this."

Kate met his eyes at last and nodded her understanding. She walked quickly up to Tyler, really not liking the fact that she had been on her own for some time. She squatted next to her, and when Tyler did not look up she rested a firm hand on her shoulder.

"Hey, Ty," she said softly. "Are you all right?"

Tyler glanced at her. She was pale and she seemed to struggle to find her words. When she did, her voice was huskier than usual, and her tone was bitter.

"RPG. Almost cut her in half," she said tersely.

"Bloody hell. Why did they aim at the compound?" Kate asked in disbelief.

Tyler just shook her head and did not reply. She stood up abruptly and faced the small group of Afghan women.

"I'm very sorry," she said.

An older woman walked up to her and started to talk quickly, crying all the while.

"I am sorry," Tyler repeated, and Kate narrowed her eyes at her, alarmed to see that she seemed close to tears.

But the Afghan woman only waved her arms and started yelling, and Kate grabbed Tyler by the wrist and pulled her away firmly.

"That's enough. It's time to go now," she said urgently, echoing Collins' earlier words.

But he was right. They had been static in the compound for too long now, and they needed to move. Tyler was well aware of this. She gripped her rifle and shook the woman off, not enough to hurt her but hard enough that she did not attempt to grab her again. She followed Kate without allowing herself another look back.

She became aware of a familiar tightening in her chest, just as she picked up the pace, heading back toward the troop. Surprised, she tried to take a deep breath, and found that she could not. Not now, damn it, she thought. She focused on her breathing and tried to slow it down, but it was too late, and she stumbled heavily on a rock. She would have hit the ground for sure if Kate had not grabbed her by the arm and held on to her.

"Just hang on a minute," she instructed, and she pulled Tyler with her against a mud wall, just before they made it back into full view of the platoon.

"There's no time," Tyler just managed to say.

"This won't take long," Kate interrupted.

She rested her hand flat on Tyler's chest to keep her in place, and she met her eyes.

"Just take a minute, and breathe."

She had noticed how pale Tyler had become, and how short of breath she appeared to be. She could recognise the early signs of a panic attack when she saw them, and there was no way Tyler was moving again until she felt certain that she was okay.

Under normal circumstances Tyler would have argued, but it was getting even harder to breathe, so she did as Kate ordered and she stayed put.

"I'm okay," she murmured for her benefit, although she was clearly not.

"Be quiet. Just breathe," Kate repeated calmly, reassuringly. "We're just going to take a minute; it's okay."

Tyler's normally laser bright eyes had turned hazy, and she realised she was having trouble focusing. She feared what was coming.

"Shit..." she murmured.

She swiped at the sweat on her brow, dipped her head slightly and breathed out. When she started to slide down against the wall Kate quickly stepped forward to support her. She slipped an arm around her waist, braced herself against the wall.

"Ty. Do I need to call for help here?" she asked anxiously.

"No, don't," Tyler panted, feeling her panic increase.

"Are you sure?"

Tyler could only nod. She was shaking, and sweat was literally pouring off her. Kate bit her lip, watching intently as the younger woman concentrated on taking deep, controlled breaths, her eyes shut tight. They were still alone. Kate would not deliberately go against Tyler's wishes, but at the same time she was prepared to call for help if the situation started to get really out of control. As it was, she was well aware that if it had been anybody else, she would have called for backup already.

She waited a little bit longer.

"Tyler," she warned then. "We need to move, now."

"Yeah..."

Tyler straightened up as she spoke. Her eyes had cleared up but she was still deathly pale. She met Kate's gaze and held on to her for a few more seconds. She found if she simply focused on Kate, if she kept her mind on her and nothing else, the panic started to recede. She stared into her dark, reassuring eyes for what seemed like an eternity, until her heart stopped its crazy beat and she was able to take a deep, full breath again.

"All right," she murmured.

Kate relaxed only a fraction. She could see in Tyler's eyes how hard it had been to regain control, and she did not want to let go of her just yet. At the same time, she knew that they had to move, and make it quick.

"You're good to go?" she simply asked.

"Yeah."

"Okay then. You lead."

Chapter Five

Later on that evening, back at base, Kate pulled a small mirror out of her medical bag and surveyed the extent of the damage. She'd live. There was a small cut, right above her eyelid, but it had not required any stitches. She would have one hell of a shiner for the next few days, but she could see okay, so she could still work and she could still go out on patrol with the teams. It was the only thing she really cared about.

Relieved as always to be back at camp, with everybody safe and well, she joined a group of young marines cooking dinner and prepared to add her own ration to the pot. The guys in the platoon often threw a few ration packs together along with a few staples, and made one big stewing pot of everything.

She sat down on a bench and smiled at a couple of them, busy sorting through a box of supplies.

"What have you got cooking tonight?" she asked.

"The boss won at cards," one of them told her, grinning. "So it's mainly chilli. With spaghetti. Again."

Kate gave a soft laugh. She could live with that.

Collins came to sit next to her, and she was glad when he put a friendly arm around her shoulders. He asked her how she was, making small talk, cracking jokes. Kate knew that the events of the afternoon had shaken him as much as they had her. It was hard when people died, even harder when kids got hit. It was nice to goof around with him for a while.

Then Tyler showed up, and Kate forgot all about the food, and all about Collins. She watched her intently as the woman made her way toward them slowly, stopping to chat and joke with some of her guys along the way. To everyone looking she looked the same as she always did, relaxed and happy, enjoying the moment, having fun with the troops.

But Kate could spot the difference a mile away.

It was not very cold, and yet Tyler was wearing a thick black fleece. Kate thought she looked a little bit pale still, and tired, and she suddenly wished they could be alone so she could find out exactly how the captain really felt. After the patrol she had disappeared inside the Ops room for the rest of the afternoon, and Kate had not had a chance to talk to her yet.

She was about to ask if she could have a quick word, when she saw Tyler bend down to retrieve a box from under a bench. She gave a quick smile when she saw that Kate was watching her, and she nodded toward the marines gathered around them.

As Kate looked up, all the guys started to sing Happy Birthday together.

Kate burst out laughing, delighted. Looking up, she accepted the box of freshly cooked pancakes from Tyler, noting the look of satisfaction in her eyes. Clearly she had wanted this to be a complete surprise, and she had definitely achieved her goal. Kate had had no idea this was coming, and she was touched that they had thought to do something to celebrate.

"How did you know it was my birthday?" she laughed.

"Asked the Intel guys, they always know everything that matters," Collins said loudly. "And here's some maple syrup to go with them. Canadian. You gonna share, right doc?"

"Of course," Kate shot back with an amused grin.

Tyler stood next to her, smiling.

"That's to make up for the black eye I gave you earlier," she said quietly.

"Thank you. And you are completely forgiven."

Tyler handed her a shoebox decorated with a little red ribbon.

"Here you go Kate. We all got you a few things."

Kate opened the box and burst out laughing again. It was full of ration pack essentials. Oreo cookies, a bar of soap, some mosquito repellent, peanut butter. Her eyes grew wide when she spotted the little bottle of Body Shop lotion.

She looked up at Tyler, who grinned and tried to look like it was nothing.

"Where did you get that?" Kate asked, amazed.

"I've been doing contraband with Bastion. Don't tell anyone."

Kate beamed at her, and she held her gaze for slightly longer than necessary. Tyler nodded, not breaking eye contact, but she took a little step back.

"I have to report to the Ops room again in five minutes, so I'll see you later okay? Enjoy your birthday treats."

She walked away quickly, ignoring Collins' knowing smile and leaving Kate to stare thoughtfully after her.

She was alone when the medic came to find her an hour later, sat in front of a couple of laptops, maps and paperwork thrown all over the table. She looked a little bit tired, seriously bored, but her eyes lit up and she smiled when she spotted Kate walking in.

"Hey birthday girl," she greeted her warmly. "How are you?"

Kate returned the smile, as always feeling herself incredibly drawn to Tyler.

"Good. What are you doing?" she asked.

Tyler glanced at the paperwork on the table.

"Sorting out insurance documents for the guys. And I have a couple of reports to finish. I'm behind on all the paperwork. Can you believe I'm having to do paperwork in a place like Cobel?"

"Well, if it helps, I saved you a couple of pancakes, and I thought you might like some coffee. Is this a good time or are you too busy?"

"Never too busy for coffee," Tyler said emphatically.

She accepted the pancakes with a smile, and wrapped her hands around the steaming mug of coffee. She took a sip and closed her eyes, sighing with pleasure.

"That's just what I needed, thank you."

She opened her eyes again and her gaze was warm when she looked at Kate.

"How is your eye now?"

"Fine. Couple of Ibuprofens did the job, and I've got perfect eye makeup for Halloween."

"That you certainly do."

"Hey. Don't push it unless you want me to give you the same look."

"You'd have to catch me first," Tyler said with a chuckle.

Kate smiled as she said that, and she watched as the handsome captain took another sip of coffee and bit into a pancake. She was laughing, but it looked like a real effort, and the way she kept blinking as if it was too hard to keep her eyes open easily betrayed her tiredness. Kate knew she could not stall any longer. She took a deep breath and asked the question she had been afraid to ask.

"So Tyler, how are you feeling?"

"Fine, thanks."

The answer was immediate and sharp.

Kate raised an eyebrow and leaned her arms on the table.

"You know I wouldn't be very good at my job if I didn't ask you about this afternoon, right?" she said.

"No... No, maybe not," Tyler agreed slowly, almost reluctantly. "But I'm fine, Kate. There is nothing to talk about."

There was a hint of wariness in her eyes as she held the medic's probing gaze, and she looked uncomfortable. She gave Kate a small smile, almost like a silent signal for her to drop the subject. But, Kate being Kate, she pushed on regardless.

"Have you had panic attacks before?"

"Look, I'm fine. Okay?"

Kate opened her mouth to argue, and then immediately thought better of it. There was no trace of the earlier smile in Tyler's eyes now, instead it had been replaced by a silent and very obvious warning.

Kate noticed when her jaw flicked. She spotted the stubbornness loaded there, and the tension in her shoulders, and she realised that she would not win this argument no matter what she said. Tyler would not budge. Incredibly, Kate found that her reaction hurt. Tyler's unwillingness to confide in her should not have hurt that much, and Kate was disturbed by the unexpected rush of emotion that suddenly made her throat tighten.

She sat back in her chair and said nothing, but her silence spoke volumes.

"So, I've got good news from Bastion," Tyler said carefully, trying to move over the unusual, awkward pause between them. "We're getting a supply drop tomorrow night. Fresh food, ammo and equipment."

"Are the medical supplies I ordered on that list of things coming as well?" Kate enquired, a little more sharply than she really intended to.

Tyler blinked, once, and her eyes darkened a little.

"I got everything you wanted doc."

"Right. Well, in this case I guess I'll see you then."

She stood up abruptly and started to walk off, but Tyler jumped up and came to stand in front of her, blocking her way.

"Hold on, Kate," she said. "Don't go off like that. Not when you're angry. Not here."

"I'm not angry. And I don't see that it matters anyway..." Kate shrugged, trying in vain to sidestep her.

"It matters to me. I know it matters to you, too."

Tyler's grey eyes flashed as she spoke. She was wide awake now. She had raised her voice and she suddenly realised how close she was to losing her temper for good. She was astounded. No one ever did that to her, no one. Yet Kate had managed to take her to that place in about two seconds flat. What the hell was going on here? She breathed deeply and got her voice under control.

"Look. What's the matter?" she said softly.

Kate took a deep breath. All she had been hoping for was an opportunity to let rip and express what she was feeling, and Tyler had left herself wide open to it.

"What's the matter is I am a doctor," she said in a low, urgent tone.

"I know. I'm just..."

"And you had a panic attack this afternoon," Kate interrupted her sharply. "It is my responsibility to address that, because if it happens again out there on patrol you could be at risk, and marines could be at risk. I don't like the fact that you are trying to brush it all under the carpet. Me included. I wasn't expecting this sort of bullshit from you, Tyler."

Tyler was silent. She just stood there, staring at Kate with a hard and serious look on her face.

"You don't know me," she murmured eventually.

Kate raised an eyebrow, taken aback by the unexpected and very odd response.

"Well. Then tell me," she said impatiently.

Tyler exhaled sharply.

"It's nothing," she muttered.

"Come on Tyler, talk to me. Is something wrong? Are you sick?"

"No. I'm fine."

"Look, you know this afternoon could have ended up badly."

"But it didn't. So just drop it please."

"I can't. I need to know what..."

"Stop it," Tyler snapped.

She looked away in frustration, and Kate bit her lower lip as she watched her expression grow even more remote and shut-down. Tyler was right in a way, she reflected worryingly. They had not known each other for long, and Kate had just pushed her pretty hard. She did not want to lose her friendship, and it was hard for her but she had to ask, she had to push. This was a battlefield after all, and her job was to make sure that everybody at Cobel was fit for duty. So that they were safe. There could be no exceptions, not even for Tyler.

In fact, especially not for her.

"Please, Tyler," she said softly.

Her tone was gentle. She reached out and touched her wrist with her fingertips.

Tyler felt her touch and struggled with a deep-seated urge to shake her off and run away, as far as she could. From the demands of a stranger, from the emotions that Kate stirred inside of her every time she insisted for more honesty, more openness, more connection.

Tyler wanted to run to protect herself, and she probably would have done exactly that, if only it had been somebody else. But there was something about Kate that stopped her. She met her eyes, and in that instant she knew that if she refused to talk to her there would be no coming back. Their friendship would be over, just like that. If there was one thing Tyler had learnt about the medic over their past few weeks together, it was that Kate would not stand for any kind of bullshit. From anyone.

Realising exactly how much her friendship with Kate meant to her was enough to give her a headache.

"Okay, if you really need to know," she mumbled.

She breathed out and looked at Kate, and Kate's legs suddenly felt weak with relief at the realisation that she had not messed up the one professional relationship that meant more to her than any she had had in a long time.

"I'm sorry doc," Tyler said simply. "I have had panic attacks before."

"Does Cox know?"

"Yes. I wouldn't be here if he didn't."

"Does he know about this afternoon too?"

"No."

"Okay. So when are you going to tell him?"

"There is no need to mention it."

Tyler was so tense she was almost shaking.

"There is no need, doc," she repeated as Kate continued to gaze at her in complete silence. "Trust me. I would tell you if it was a problem, and it's not."

Kate waited her out for a couple of seconds, but Tyler remained silent this time, and eventually Kate nodded slowly. She had many more questions to ask, but she realised that this would have to do for now. Despite her even tone of voice Tyler looked very upset, and almost like she was about to cry, and Kate wished there was something she could have said or done to help her. Anything. If only she knew what.

"Thank you for being honest with me," she said, at a loss for words, and Tyler just shrugged and looked away again.

Kate hesitated.

"I'm sorry," she said. "I know you're angry with me..."

"I'm not angry. You're just doing your job."

"This is not about the job," Kate countered, and immediately wondered if it had been such a wise thing to tell Tyler. She sighed in frustration. To hell with it.

"I care about you, Ty. Okay? That's why. And you scared me this afternoon."

Once again the heartfelt emotion in her voice, the genuine concern, tore at Tyler's heart.

"It won't happen again," she said roughly.

She shrugged a little and this time she maintained eye contact.

"I haven't had one of those panic attacks in nearly eight months now. I kind of thought it was all behind me."

Without thinking, Kate grabbed hold of her arms with both hands and pulled her closer to her. Tyler was too cold.

"If you don't feel well," she said urgently, "then talk to me, okay? Nobody else needs to know, and nobody will, I promise. But if anything happened to you out on patrol, I just…"

She stopped abruptly and dropped her hands. She realised at once that she had no words to explain how she would feel if anything happened to Tyler. She just could not bear to think about it, and it had absolutely nothing whatsoever to do with the job. She breathed out and gave a little shake of the head.

"I'm fine. And nothing is going to happen Kate," Tyler said confidently.

Kate gave her a heartfelt smile.

"I will hold you to that, captain," she said fiercely.

For a few seconds they just stared into each other's eyes.

"I told Collins I would do circuits with him and the guys tonight," Kate said eventually, reluctantly. "So I've got to go get sweaty again."

Tyler smiled a little.

"Sweaty can be fun," she said without conviction.

"Are you coming?"

"Better not. I still have a lot of work to do here."

"Anything I can help you with?"

"No, but thanks."

Tyler smiled tiredly.

"You go put the boys through their paces doc. I'm fine."

She watched Kate go, suddenly aware that she was trembling. She dropped onto her chair and leaned her elbows on the table, slowly running both hands through her hair. She stared numbly into space as she thought of the way Kate had just stood up to her. Because she cared. Tyler felt her face heat up as she remembered her exact words. *I care about you, Ty.*

She suspected there would be more questions. She was not sure exactly how she would deal with those, if and when they came. Yet a part of her wanted to believe that whatever Kate asked, and whatever Tyler revealed about herself, it would be okay.

She remembered talking to one of the psychiatrists at Camp Pendleton, a marine like her. Yet she had not trusted him. She had held back and told him exactly what he expected to hear. Turns out he could not have cared less anyway. He went through the motions, cleared her for active duty, and two days later she had landed at Kandahar. Since then there had been no panic attacks.

Until today.

Chapter Six

"How many confirmed KIA?"

Kate ran into the Ops Room tent a week later just as the company commander asked the question.

KIA. Killed In Action.

Major Tim Cox nodded in her direction when he spotted her, his sea- blue eyes preoccupied, his mind obviously fully on the conversation he was having with the patrol commander currently out in the field. Kate nodded at him, and she quickly scanned the room until she spotted Tyler, standing up at the back of the tent, oblivious to what was going on around them, busy studying a bunch of maps on the table. Safe.

"One confirmed KIA," the tense reply came over the radio. "We have three Cat B coming in as well."

"You got that doctor?" Cox enquired, glancing toward Kate again, this time his full attention on her.

"Yes sir. We're ready for them. Lieutenant Thomson is already talking to Bastion about extraction," Kate added, referring to her colleague Rich.

Matt was out on R&R in Kandahar. It would fall to the two remaining medics to treat the wounded and make sure they were ready for transport back to Bastion. Cat B wounded meant that the soldiers' injuries were life threatening. Kate felt worried and extremely on edge, but absolutely ready to do the best she could do with the resources she had. If she had to, she would even make them up.

Tyler looked up sharply when she heard her voice, her grey eyes focusing on her with the familiar intensity that Kate had come to expect. Tyler was always that little bit more switched on, that little bit more intense than everybody else seemed to be. Especially when Kate was around.

"I'm with you doc," she volunteered straight away.

"Keep me posted," Cox said to her as she ran out with Kate.

"What happened?" Kate asked as they made their way quickly toward the medical tent.

She had been in bed grabbing some sleep after a long patrol when she was called back out again. Six hours on her feet and one major contact during that patrol, but no casualties on their side and a few Taliban weapons seized and destroyed. Kate had been looking forward to a few hours of sleep, but it was not to be.

"A troop of British Marines were out with members of the ANA about five miles from here when they got ambushed," Tyler explained, walking fast. "The ANA chief got killed, and three of the marines got injured in an RPG blast. We sent a bunch of our guys out to help bring them back, they should be here in ten minutes."

Kate nodded, her mind on the task ahead of her.

"Okay. We'll be ready for them when they come in."

"Is there anything I can help you with out here?" Tyler asked, stopping abruptly just outside the tent.

Kate looked at her and did not reply straight away.

Tyler was still wearing her patrol kit, minus her Bergen, and she had her weapon in hand. She was still dusty and sweaty from their earlier outing, and Kate suddenly realised that she must have been busy in a debrief all that time. She felt guilty that she had managed a shower and a lie down when Tyler had obviously been up and working all the while.

"Are you going straight back out again?" she asked in dismay.

"Yeah. I'm going out to help secure the LZ with the guys. Unless you need me here."

"I think we should be fine."

"Okay."

Tyler gave her a quick nod and started to walk away.

"I'll see you later doc. Good luck, okay?"

"Hang on just a second, Ty."

Kate ran inside the medical tent and came back out with a bottle of Lucozade.

"Drink this."

Tyler grabbed the bottle with a grateful smile.

"Thanks. I'm on fire."

"Bet you haven't eaten either?"

"Haven't had time."

Kate narrowed her eyes at her as she suddenly spotted the faint shadows under her eyes, which were not normally that obvious. She put a hand on her shoulder and dropped her voice.

"Are you feeling all right?"

Tyler shrugged.

"Sure. Just a long day at the office is all."

Kate observed her for a second longer. There had been no repeats of the panic attack and no signs that Tyler was unwell in any way. Yet Kate had been on red alert ever since that day.

Tyler slipped on her sunglasses and made a face.

"Stop fretting doc, I'm fine," she said.

Kate smiled a little.

"Sorry. I'm not going all dramatic on you I swear."

Tyler gave a soft chuckle and drained the rest of the Lucozade.

"Hope not."

"Be careful."

"Always."

For the next fifty minutes Kate did not think of anything except the three lives which were in her hands. She and David managed to stabilise the wounded Royal Marines, and as the guys flew out of Cobel on the rescue helicopter Kate felt certain that they stood a good chance, thanks to their work.

She spent an hour cleaning their equipment afterwards whilst David did a thorough inventory of everything they had used and everything they would need to replace.

Once this was done she walked back to the Ops tent for a quick word with Major Cox.

Then she was on her own time once more.

It was nearly five in the afternoon by then and getting dark, and she immediately went in search of Tyler. She tried the kitchen before going to their tent, and as she opened the flap to walk inside Collins stormed past her, looking angry and almost knocking her over. He did not stop to talk or apologise. Frowning, Kate walked in, and immediately noticed that Tyler looked upset.

"Hey. What's up?" she asked, concerned.

Tyler glanced at her and sighed a little. Kate seemed to have this uncanny knack for always appearing at the most awkward of times, she reflected.

"We had some bad news today," she said. "Don't worry about it."

But Kate narrowed her eyes at her, instantly worried.

"Bad news from home?" she asked.

"Yes."

"What happened?"

"A marine I served with," Tyler explained reluctantly. "One of Ben's friends. He killed himself yesterday."

"Bloody hell, Tyler," Kate murmured.

She immediately sat down close to her, wrapped her arm around her waist and held on tight.

"I'm sorry sweetheart. What happened?"

Tyler's mind stumbled on the word. Sweetheart? she thought. Since when? But it felt good, and she unconsciously allowed herself to lean against Kate a little more.

"His name was Gary. He was thirty two," she said. "Got

wounded on tour a year ago, left the Marines, started drinking. He was arrested on DUI a couple of times. There was some fighting in bars... His wife left him. I guess everything got too much for him eventually."

"Were you close?"

"We'd been on tour together. You know."

"Of course."

"And it reminded me of someone else that I..."

Tyler realised she was on the verge of revealing way too much. Her voice suddenly caught in her throat and she quickly looked away, but not before Kate could spot the flash of emotion in her eyes.

She frowned and opened her mouth to speak.

"Anyway," Tyler carried on quickly, before Kate had a chance to say anything. "Gary was really good friends with Ben. I just told him the news, and he didn't take it very well."

"Where is he now?"

Tyler shrugged a little.

"Out working it out of his system I guess," she said in a low voice.

Kate nodded quietly, watching her.

"What about you?" she asked.

"Me what?"

"How will you work it out of your system?"

Tyler turned her head to look at her. Kate was so close to her. If she had moved her head only a little bit she would have been able to kiss her. Where the hell that thought had come from she had no idea. But the woman's fingers felt red hot against her wrist, and Tyler felt her face heat up all of a sudden.

She blinked a couple of times.

"Don't need to," she murmured.

Kate reflected that there were several things she could have said in answer to Tyler's comment, none helpful in their current situation.

She shifted a little and relaxed her grip on her. When she did she noted the quick spark of frustration mixed with unconscious relief in Tyler's eyes, and she did not know exactly what it meant.

"If you say so," she said quietly.

Tyler's gaze clouded over like a hurricane coming, and she nodded a little, seemingly lost in her own thoughts. Not good ones.

"Yeah," she said hoarsely.

She suddenly realised how badly she wanted Kate to touch her again. She felt cold all of a sudden, felt the separation, and she struggled to maintain her composure.

"Hey. You still with me?" Kate asked.

Tyler twitched.

"Yeah, sorry. Just a bit distracted that's all."

She was taken aback when Kate moved behind her without warning and rested her hands on her shoulders. Tyler tensed up. Had the woman been reading her mind?

"What are you doing?" she asked, suddenly worried.

"Helping you. Relax."

"I don't need help, I'm fine."

Kate gave a soft laugh as she moved her hands over the rigid muscles in Tyler's shoulders.

"I'd say you need a lot of help actually," she remarked. "You're so tight I'm surprised you can even move your head."

She pressed her thumbs into a particularly hard knot at the base of her neck, and kept on it even when Tyler squirmed uncomfortably under her touch.

"Ow, Kate, that hurts."

"Shh. Stay still. I need to get this one."

She applied pressure until she felt the painful spot soften, and rubbed her palm in small circles over it.

"How's that? Just pressure now, no pain?"

Tyler had closed her eyes.

"Hmm, yeah," she mumbled. "Just pressure."

Kate nodded and lowered her hands a little more.

"Let me do this," she murmured. "Okay?"

"I need to go find Ben..."

"I know, but it won't take long, Ty. You won't be any good to anybody around here if you end up getting injured yourself, all right? Lie down."

Tyler hesitated, but she reckoned a couple of minutes would not hurt, and it was hard to walk away. She knew she was kidding herself that this was only a case of tight shoulder muscles keeping her in place.

But she was too tired to fight it.

"Okay then," she murmured as she lay on the bed and rested her head on her folded arms. "Five minutes, doc."

"Yes, captain."

The more she got to know Tyler the more Kate realised that there were two clear sides to her personality. One was her professional armour, calm, solid, confident. The one everyone got to experience when Tyler was out on patrol or working with her troops. That side of her which left no one in any doubt that when things got tight and dangerous, they could look to Tyler for strength and direction. She would only let them see what she wanted them to see, that she was a leader, an invincible soldier, not a vulnerable woman made of simple flesh and blood.

Kate was pretty sure not many people, if any, were ever allowed to see past her barriers, through the carefully constructed shield of her professional excellence. The other side of Tyler, the one that Kate herself had only caught a few fleeting impressions of, was alive and kicking behind her walls. There was a sadness there, heavy, profound and undiluted. Intense and dangerous, waiting patiently for its moment to strike.

Kate did not know what it meant, who or what had put it there, but she worried that at some point in the near future it might become too difficult for Tyler to control it. The panic attack not that long ago had been a clear warning of that, and as she carried on with her gentle massage she wondered how long it would take before Tyler collapsed under the weight of her emotions. Hopefully never, she thought. But she was worried about her. If and when it happened, front-line Afghanistan would be no place for a breakdown.

Kate glanced down at her now as the officer shifted a little, her eyes still closed and her body a lot more relaxed now.

She felt an almost irresistible urge to lie down next to her, to take her in her arms, to protect her against whatever was responsible for that mysterious flash of painful emotion she got in her eyes sometimes.

Instead she gave her a pat on the arm and a gentle push.

"Here you go captain," she announced, rather more loudly than she intended to, hoping that it would help to dispel the multitude of questions bumping around her head, all those ones she absolutely knew Tyler would not want her to ask. "Bit better now?"

Tyler sat up slowly. It was a real effort to get moving again. Kate's touch had been a mixture of strength and tenderness, gentle yet powerful.

When Kate touched her, Tyler felt at peace.

"Better," she murmured. "Thanks doc."

Kate stared at her as Tyler glanced away, and waited until she turned to meet her eyes again.

"Sure?" she asked.

Tyler gave her a firm nod and she attempted a smile, but the shadows in her eyes were so pronounced Kate knew for sure it was a lie. An unconscious one maybe, but still a lie. This was a woman who was completely lost at sea and did not even have a clue she needed help. Kate leaned a little closer against her, and rested her hand gently against the side of her face.

"Come back anytime," she said.

Tyler's eyes almost closed under the soft caress, and then there was some loud noise outside, voices close by. Tyler flinched as if she had suddenly slammed back down inside her body. She stood up and for a second struggled to find her balance.

"Thanks doc," she said again.

"Well, it is my job to look after the troops and make sure they are fit for duty," Kate said dryly. "Hey. You need to rest more."

Tyler shrugged a little but did not comment.

"I need to go," she said.

"So you said."

"See you later doc?"

"I'll be here. Be careful."

"Always."

Kate nodded, and Tyler grabbed her rifle and walked out into the night.

"So did you kiss her or what?"

"No!" Tyler exclaimed. "It's the third time you asked me that, give it a rest will you!"

"What the hell is wrong with you Tyler?"

"Shut up."

She had gone out to find Collins, scoured the whole of the compound until she finally came upon him sat on his own at the back of the shower block. Now he seemed intent on pissing her off and sticking his nose into her business.

Pretty much his usual self then, she reflected moodily.

He gave a wild laugh as Tyler shook her head in annoyance, and slapped her hard on the shoulder.

"You might as well, buddy," he remarked darkly. "Could be dead tomorrow."

"Thanks. That's a cheerful thought after such a fucked up day."

"You know I'm right. I've seen the way you two look at each other."

Tyler stared at him as he drank from a flask, grimaced as whatever was in it burnt its way down his throat.

"To Gary," he said roughly.

"To Gary," Tyler repeated. "Hey, do you even give a shit that you are drinking in front of your superior officer?"

"No. Should I?"

Tyler smiled in spite of herself.

"Not tonight. Special circumstances," she said.

"I'm sorry that Gary's suicide reminded you of Helen," Ben said, and he took another sip.

He did not offer to share with Tyler. He knew she never touched alcohol. He felt her stiffen as he mentioned the name of her ex, and was not very surprised when she remained silent. He felt her grow rigid next to him, and he sighed.

"Do you miss her?" he asked, his tone more gentle this time.

Tyler shook her head.

"No," she said sharply, wondering how it was possible that even after three years, the simple mention of Helen's name was enough to make her break into a cold sweat.

"Does she remind you of her?"

"Who?"

"The doc. Does she remind you of Helen?"

Tyler stretched her legs out in front of her and rested her head against the wall. She felt herself grow warm and relaxed as she thought of the British medic, with her gentle yet uncompromising ways.

She thought of the way Kate made her feel and she wanted to smile.

"No," she said firmly. "Kate is nothing like Helen."

It was Collins' turn to look at her. He had known Tyler for five years, worked with her for three. He had witnessed the carnage that had followed the end of her relationship with Helen.

"Kate is okay, buddy," he said. "Not some fucking crazy bitch."

"Hey," Tyler snapped.

"What? I'm right and you know it."

"I know it, I don't necessarily want to hear you say it."

He smiled.

"So."

"So what?"

"Are you going to kiss her or what? Cos I will if you don't."

Tyler lowered her head and she started to laugh.

"Good luck with that," she snorted.

Chapter Seven

Kate was awake early the following day. She remained still for a little while, her eyes closed, enjoying the feeling of being warm and safe inside her sleeping bag for a few more minutes.

More and more she was finding life difficult at Cobel. She knew she had lost her drive. She was still as dedicated to the soldiers under her care as she had always been, but she wanted to go home now. Too many years in too many war zones, and all she wanted now was to feel safe. She remembered what Tyler had said about not knowing why they were there anymore, and feeling fed up sometimes. Kate felt the same way. But she was getting out after this tour, and Tyler had not said anything about leaving.

Stretching lazily, Kate turned over when she felt movement on her right, and she found her tent mate already up and pulling on a pair of shorts and a black Skins top.

Kate watched her, her eyes lingering over the sleek muscles in her legs. Tyler looked up and caught her staring.

"Hey, morning," she said softly. "Sorry about the noise."

"That's okay, I wasn't sleeping."

Kate burrowed deeper inside her sleeping bag, watching Tyler as she reached for her running shoes.

"I'm going for a run. You want to come?"

"Shit. I knew you were going to ask me that."

Tyler shook her head with a grin.

"This is not compulsory."

Kate groaned.

"No, I'm coming," she said firmly.

She dressed quickly, brushed her teeth and followed Tyler out of the tent.

"Wow, look at this," Tyler exclaimed in surprise as they stepped out.

She stopped and glanced at Kate, her face lit up by a brilliant and completely delighted smile.

"I don't know about you, but I was not expecting this."

Everywhere was quiet out, and the entire camp was coated in a thick layer of frost. It looked just like snow. And it made everything appear very pretty and peaceful.

Kate filled her lungs with crisp, clean morning air, and she allowed herself to rest a friendly arm around Tyler's shoulders.

"Looks like home," she said softly. "It's beautiful."

Tyler nodded and remained still, breathing slowly, a little bewildered at how good Kate's embrace felt. She knew it was a completely innocent touch, the simple need to be close. She looked at the medic, gave her a smile and returned the friendly hold. It felt like the most natural thing in the world when Kate turned to face her then, and wrapped her arms around her neck.

Tyler closed her eyes, and her brain switched itself off all by itself.

"You smell nice," she murmured.

"It's the Body Shop lotion you gave me."

"Oh yeah? That's nice."

Kate tightened her grip on Tyler and ran her fingers along the back of her neck, enjoying the feel of soft, hot skin beneath her fingertips. The touch was too gentle and deliberate to be anything but a caress. Yet Tyler did not move. Kate let her fingers drift up into her hair, and she smiled.

"You're nice, captain," she said softly.

Tyler took a deep breath and shifted a little closer still. She got a sudden flash of home in California, and the small path that led down to the beach and the ocean. She got a glimpse of Kate walking ahead of her on the beach, turning round to smile at her, opening her arms to her.

Startled, she let go.

Kate said nothing but she gave her a lingering look. She looked sad, and Tyler felt concern for her all of a sudden.

"What's wrong, Kate?" she asked.

Kate gave a little shrug and sighed.

"Nothing," she said. "Just feeling a bit homesick, that's all."

Tyler's expression grew pensive.

"I know," she said gently. "But you haven't got long to go now, right? You'll be home in no time."

"Yes. But what about you?"

Tyler hesitated.

"Well, I'm doing back to back tours, so..."

Kate winced and averted her eyes quickly. She should have known. The thought that she would go home and leave Tyler behind in deadly Helmand was not something she wanted to dwell on just now. Or discuss.

Tyler seemed to read her mind.

"Can I help change your mood?" she asked.

Kate raised an eyebrow, and her eyes sparkled in anticipation.

"You certainly can. Taking me back to bed?" she said hopefully.

Tyler burst out laughing.

"Nope!" she exclaimed. "Taking you for a run. Works every time. Come on, doc!"

The compound was approximately the size of two football fields put together, and as Kate quickly found out, more than enough for Tyler to take her mind off things in a way that only a true runner would enjoy. Which Kate definitely was not. They warmed up slowly, and then picked up the pace for the next twenty minutes, staying close to the inside walls. Tyler chatted away happily for most of the run, while Kate struggled to get enough breath to keep up with her.

"Enjoying it?" Tyler asked at one point.

"Enjoying is not the word," Kate gasped, earning herself an encouraging pat on the shoulder.

"Nearly done. Stay with me!" Tyler instructed.

And then she flashed her a little grin, and took off ahead of Kate.

The medic was not one to get dropped easily though. She gritted her teeth, focused, and managed to keep up with Tyler for the final few minutes, even giving her a sprint as they finished. She was feeling rather ecstatic when they finally slowed down to an easy jog, heading back to their tent across the compound.

"Oh, boy, remind me not to do that again," she exclaimed, struggling to catch her breath.

Tyler glanced at her, smiling, noting the look of utter relief on her friend's face.

"Well done!" she told her, laughing. "I take it running isn't your thing then?"

"Not hard to spot. Yes, I hate it," Kate admitted.

Tyler shot her an admiring look.

"You're very good, especially considering that you don't like it," she remarked. "What's your favourite sport?"

"I like to row," Kate replied. "Get you in a boat, and I can show you some real pain," she added with a mischievous little smile.

"Guess I'm lucky the Helmand river is out of bounds then, uh?"

"Yes, You have no idea!"

Tyler laughed and turned to stretch, and Kate touched her shoulder lightly.

"Did you get to speak to Ben last night?" she asked.

"Yes."

"And is he okay?"

"Yeah, he's good. Thanks Kate."

"And you?"

"I'm good too," Tyler assured her.

She bent over to grab her ankles, and Kate sighed.

"You can say that again," she muttered.

"What?"

Kate blushed, but she was saved from answering by one of the guys from 2 platoon running toward them. Tyler's expression changed immediately, and her eyes hardened a little as he came to a stop near them.

"You're needed in the Ops room right away, captain," the man informed her.

Kate watched Tyler run off with him, feeling the familiar tension in the pit of her stomach. Something dodgy was going on. Deciding against a much needed shower, she went into their tent instead and changed quickly into her patrol kit, pretty certain that they would be going out shortly. Then she went to join the other medics, and waited for news.

She was losing track of time at Cobel, her life revolving around food, exercise, treating the locals, and intensely stressful outings where the marines tried to draw out the Taliban, and for the most part, succeeded.

On paper their mission was a hearts and minds campaign. And it was. But as Tyler had explained to her bluntly one day, their other objective here was to kill as many of them as possible, until one day they either left for good, or there were not enough of them left to plant IEDs. Then the farmers could start moving around freely again, the villages could start to rebuild their markets and places of work, and children and coalition soldiers could stop being blown up.

"Bit of a suicide mission, don't you think?" Kate remembered asking.

Tyler had simply shrugged.

"We are tasked to disrupt. So this is what we do. Most of the times we win."

But today their luck had turned. 3 platoon were stuck on the edge of the green zone, fighting a group of about thirty rebels, and they had taken a couple of casualties. Air support were busy helping a group of Royal Marines thirty miles away and would not be able to divert to their position quickly. Tyler's troop was being sent out to provide additional fire power. Suicide mission or not, Kate was in on it. And so just over forty five minutes later she found herself right in the middle of a huge contact.

Two guys had been shot, one in the leg, but he was stable. The other one had lost his thumb. He too would be okay. But shortly after Kate got on site, she heard the dreaded shout of "medic" once more.

Ducking and zigzagging so she did not get shot herself, she quickly made her way to the injured soldier. She gasped when she saw the size of the hole in his neck. She recognised him instantly. It was Sam, one of the guys she had met on her first day. He was from Chicago, and his mother was from York. He had chatted to Kate happily about her hometown, and revealed that he was also into rowing. This was his first tour of duty.

Adrenaline flashed hot and cold through Kate as she assessed him quickly. She could see his artery had been severely damaged, but if she could stop the flow of blood and the Chinook was quick enough he still had a chance.

She got on top of him and dug her knee into his wound.

"Tyler!" she called.

"Right here, Kate."

Tyler was right behind her, as always. It did not matter how many things she had to get right when out on patrol, what busy and complicated mission parameters she had to coordinate, she never strayed too far away from Kate. She always kept a close eye on her to make sure that she stayed safe.

Kate was well aware of it, and if any of the guys had behaved that way with her she would have resented it. But she liked to keep a close eye on Tyler as well, and so she was happy to let her think she was getting away with it.

"What can I do?" the captain asked.

She appeared calm, and her voice was controlled as always, but she took one look at the injured soldier and all colour left her face.

"Grab some tape in my bag, we need to pack the wound and stop this bleeding," Kate told her.

"Okay."

"GET DOWN!"

Kate heard the warning as the same time that Collins knocked her roughly to the ground. Bullets were flying, kicking the dirt all around them. When Kate glanced up she saw that Tyler was now on top of the injured man, lying on top of him with her elbow in his neck. Her full attention was on him, and she appeared to be totally oblivious to what was going on around them.

Fear squeezed its hand around Kate's throat.

Next to her, Collins lay on his stomach returning fire like a madman.

"Monster call sign, Monster call sign," he was yelling on his radio at the same time, "we need all your firepower on grid reference 250835."

His voice was drowned out by the roar of an F-16 jet fighter flying above them. It flew low and hard and aimed his weapons at the grid reference Collins had just given them. Kate did not stop to watch the rest of it.

She crawled back to Tyler and her casualty.

"Will you get down!" she exclaimed.

"I can't stop the bleeding, Kate," Tyler replied anxiously.

"Let me do it. You get me some tape."

Kate grabbed her by the wrist as she was crawling away, and looked deep into her eyes.

"Watch yourself," she ordered.

Tyler nodded and disappeared. She was back with the tape after a few seconds, and Kate took it from her and started packing the wound. She worked quickly, but she made sure that the job was done properly. She was aware that the shooting seemed to have stopped, and in the distance she recognised the sound of a rescue Chinook approaching. Tyler was kneeling next to her, waiting, her face pale as she watched her wounded colleague. Her eyes were unusually unfocused and distant, and Kate did not like to see that look on her face. She gripped her shoulder and flashed her a reassuring smile.

"Hey. He has a good chance, okay? I need to talk to the medics on the Chinook."

Tyler shook herself.

"Sure, I'll put you on."

Kate filled the crew in, making sure that they were ready for transfusion and got as much blood ready as they could.

"Sam, can you hear me buddy?"

Collins was talking to the casualty now. The man was barely conscious but Collins was talking to him, his face intense, his mouth close to his ear. "Think of Melissa and the kids, okay?" Kate heard him say. "You fall asleep now you won't wake up again, you understand? You stay awake, buddy, I'm not fucking kidding."

They all ducked as the Chinook landed, and once more Kate found herself running back to the helicopter alongside the stretcher, yelling stats and instructions at the crew.

"Keep him alive, guys!" was the last thing that she said to them, and one of the medics on board gave her a thumbs up and a confident grin.

Then she got blasted with debris and mud again as the Chinook took off hard and disappeared, and silence followed.

For the first time then things calmed down a little and Kate realised that it had started to rain. Pretty soon the weather was so bad she could barely see five meters in front of her. She could make out Tyler and Collins not too far away, deep in conversation. Everybody else had gone firm in a circle around them, and every single marine in the troop looked alert and ready to fire. The rain made no difference to them. One of their people had been hit, and their collective anger was palpable in the air.

Kate realised that she had never felt so tired. Belatedly she remembered that Tyler had shoved a Powerbar in her jacket pocket before they left, and she reached for it and started eating. It tasted like cardboard, but she had to keep her strength up. When Tyler's voice came on the radio she felt a sudden urge to cry. She wanted her near. She wanted to be able to touch her and know that she was okay. She did not know where those feelings were coming from, but she felt overwhelmed by them. Kate brushed at her eyes, and she took a few deep breaths to steady herself.

She had to stay focused. Now was not the time to fold.

"Guys, we're leaving," Tyler announced suddenly. "Keep your eyes open and cover your arcs. Let's go."

Kate stood up and prepared to move off. It was freezing cold and after just about five minutes she found that she was struggling to keep up with the pace. She wished she had stayed in bed now instead of going running earlier. Tyler was up in front, just ahead of her, and she was crashing through the fields at a crazy sort of speed. Everyone was struggling.

It took them only thirty-five minutes to get back, five excruciating miles zigzagging through a maze of flooded fields. They could not use proper paths, or roads, for fear of stepping onto an IED. Similarly, they could not go back the exact same way that they had come in the morning.

It was as if Tyler had chosen the most difficult, treacherous route she could possibly find. But it paid off. They did not encounter any IEDs. And no one took a shot at them.

Kate felt dizzy with exhaustion by the time they made it back. She dropped her Bergen on the ground as soon as she knew she was safe, and she bent over, hands on her knees, struggling to catch her breath. What the hell was wrong with her today, she wondered. She was not a runner all right, but still she could not understand why she was feeling so out of it.

"Kate."

She looked up at the sound of Tyler's voice. She smiled weakly, noting that Tyler did not look the slightest bit tired. Soaked to the skin, muddy, cold, yes. But not tired. In fact she appeared to be vibrating with some secret energy, and she looked very beautiful. Her eyes were burning, and when she spoke her voice shook a little.

No secret energy, Kate realised then, just too much adrenaline. This was not necessarily a good thing.

"I just spoke to base," Tyler informed her. "Sam is still touch and go, but he's a fit guy and they really think that he is going to make it. You did great out there today Kate," she added with feeling.

"Thanks..."

Tyler frowned.

"Are you okay? You look really pale."

"Fine," Kate reassured her quickly. "Just hungry I guess."

"Right. I need to speak to the guys before they stand down and I have to go through debrief. You go take a shower, get into some dry clothes and warm up. I'll catch up with you later."

Kate nodded, too tired to talk, and Tyler was gone in an instant.

Chapter Eight

Two hours later it was her turn to face the dreaded shower. Solar panels or not, the water these days was pretty much always cold. At least they had some, she reflected, as always trying to focus on the positive. She stood under the icy trickle of water and gritted her teeth, her thoughts on the events of the last few hours.

She was feeling hot, burning rage at the thought that one of her men had nearly been killed again. Somehow she would have liked nothing better than if the Taliban had tried to attack them on the way back. She had been ready for a fight, desperate for one even, and the run back had not even made a dent in her. She was still consumed with adrenaline, and as she stared at her hands she realised that she was shaking. Suddenly concerned, she took several deep breaths, closed her eyes and concentrated on calming down.

Get a grip Tyler, she thought angrily. No time for panic or nerves out here. She was angry with herself enough as it was, having lost it in front of Kate the other day.

She washed herself and washed her hair, twice, getting rid of mud and blood in record time. Once she had put on clean fatigues and a warm, thick fleece she started to feel better. She put on clean socks and her boots back on, glad that it had stopped raining. She needed a hot drink, and to find Kate.

Kate, who had been on her mind all day.

Tyler walked quickly toward their tent, reflecting on how quickly she had gotten used to having the medic around with her, pretty much all of the time. She felt a little bit out of sync when she could not see her, when she did not know where she was. She felt incredibly easy around Kate, and she was getting used to the way the woman always seemed to want to touch her, hold her, as if just being close was never enough. She was doing it too much. A few times Tyler had caught her eyes on her, seen tenderness reflected in her expression. If she could see it then everybody else probably could as well. And Tyler knew she had to be careful.

As for herself, she liked the way Kate behaved with her a little too much. She could not afford to get used to it. If nothing else, Kate would be gone soon.

Still, Tyler had started to wonder how it would feel to kiss her, and touch her. It was not a side of her life which Tyler normally chose to pay much attention to. She purposely avoided intimate relationships, and as a Marines officer who spent months at a time away from home in war zones across the world, working with men who she did not fancy, she was lucky that her career made being single the easiest option of all.

But with Kate, recently, she had been reminded of these feelings. Sometimes she wanted to hold her, and be held by her. And talk. For hours. Just nothing else. She had not felt that in years, and she did not want to feel those things ever again, despite Collins' well-meaning advice the previous night.

Irritated once more for not being able to control her thoughts, Tyler ducked into her tent and found it empty. She walked to the kitchen area and looked around impatiently, frowning.

"Hey Lenster, you seen the doc anywhere?" she asked.

"Hey boss. Not tonight, no. Hey, I was kind of hoping I could dig into your stash of chocolate ," he added hopefully.

"Knock yourself out," Tyler muttered, and she started to walk away. Pretty much immediately though she caught herself, and turned back to smile at him.

"How're you doing buddy?" she asked. "Okay?"

He gave her a grateful smile and nodded.

"Yeah boss."

"Good."

"I just hope those guys got destroyed by the jet like you said."

"I believe he got them. If not, we will. Throw me a couple of Sneakers bars and feel free to share the rest of it with the guys."

Armed with the right kind of supplies, Tyler's next stop was the medical tent. She walked in and looked around, instantly worried when she did not see Kate.

"Kate!" she called loudly.

"Right here, Ty…"

Tyler spun around and stared.

"Hey. What are you doing on the floor?" she asked. "It's freezing in here."

She walked over to where Kate sat, her back against a row of folded stretchers, paperwork spread out all around her on the thick floor cover.

"Just catching up on some work. I was going to come and find you."

"Found you first. What's up doc?"

"I need your help with something."

"Okay." Tyler nodded and sat cross-legged in front of Kate. "You look exhausted," she observed.

"I am. I knew I should have stayed in bed this morning. This running thing you do is definitely not for me." Kate caught Tyler's right hand in hers and gave her a small smile. "You, on the other hand, look really gorgeous," she said simply.

Tyler gazed at her in silence for a couple of seconds, surprised at the unusual compliment and resisting the urge to simply pull her into her arms. She noticed how pale she looked, how Kate seemed to be struggling to keep her eyes open. Something was off. Kate did not just look tired, she looked ill. Then Tyler's gaze drifted down to her sleeve, and she narrowed her eyes at the tiny droplets of blood dripping from it.

"What the hell… Kate."

"Yeah."

"Are you hurt?"

Kate exhaled slowly, and to Tyler's amazement she nodded yes.

"That's why I was going to come and find you," she repeated. "It's nothing much but it needs stitches."

Past the initial moment of shock, when her heart nearly jumped out of her chest, Tyler felt instantly angry, almost let down.

"For God's sake, why didn't you tell me?" she demanded, her eyes wide in disbelief.

"Because I didn't know myself," Kate answered calmly. "Honest. I only realised when I was in the shower. Then I put a bandage on it but it seems to be leaking…"

She tried to shrug it off and winced in pain as she did. Tyler's anger disappeared in an instant, replaced instead by a low simmering fear, coming from somewhere deep inside her. Earlier on that afternoon she had had her arm inside a colleague's open neck wound trying to stop him from bleeding to death, and now Kate was bleeding too. That was way too close for comfort. The back of her neck nearly seized up with tension, and panic forced its way inside her chest. She had to take a deep breath to stop herself from getting dizzy.

She had to do something.

"Okay, let's get you up," she said quickly.

She leaned forward and wrapped both arms around Kate's waist.

"Hold on to me," she instructed.

"Watch your back, I'm heavy…"

"Do I look like I'm weak? Come on, hold on to me."

Kate wrapped her good arm around Tyler's neck, feeling a little bit faint as the captain pulled her up with her slowly. She swayed a little in spite of herself and gritted her teeth. Her arm really did hurt and she was feeling dizzy.

"Okay?" Tyler asked quietly.

Kate nodded at the same time as her legs trembled. For a second she thought she might simply pass out, and she held tighter onto Tyler.

"Are you okay?" Tyler repeated, and her voice was thick with worry.

"A little faint," Kate murmured. "Just don't let go, okay?"

Tyler shook her head and held her harder.

"Of course not," she said.

She walked Kate to one of the camp beds and helped her to sit down on it. She kept a hand safely on her back in case she should fall.

"Okay, now show me," she said.

Kate slipped her arm out of her sleeve, again wincing as she moved it.

"It looks a lot worse than it is," she warned as Tyler slipped on a pair of gloves.

"Sure," Tyler muttered, unconvinced.

Carefully, she unwrapped the bloody bandage, and Kate watched her expression darken as she saw what was underneath.

"Oh, Kate," she murmured in dismay.

"It's all right, Ty."

"No. No it isn't. Not even close."

"I think I got hit just as Collins knocked me to the ground. Might have been worse if he hadn't."

"And you didn't feel anything?" Tyler asked with a shake of the head.

"Maybe I did... I'm not sure. Too many things going on all at once I guess. But it's just a graze, nothing serious."

"It's deep, Kate," Tyler stated with a quick glance at her.

Her eyes were dark with concern.

"And it's bleeding too. Damn! I can't believe I didn't notice it when we were out."

"As I recall you had quite a few other things to worry about at the time. Can you stitch me up?"

"I think so. I've done it before. But don't you want David to do it?"

"No. I want you to do it," Kate said in a low voice. "Please. Is that okay?"

She did not want anybody else near her right now. Only Tyler. The captain looked closely at her, saw tears shining in her eyes before Kate blinked them away quickly.

"Of course," she said gently. "I'll do it, no problem. Do you need pain killers before I start? A local anaesthetic or something?"

"Already had some of that," Kate replied tiredly.

Tyler followed her gaze to a discarded syringe set on the table, and she could not help but smile a little.

"You know, Kate, you don't have to do everything yourself in this place. We're a team."

"I know. You and me. So that's why you're going to do the stitching."

With a quick shake of the head, Tyler set to work. It took seven stitches, and when she finished she exhaled softly and shook the tension out of her arm. She glanced at Kate, whose intense brown eyes had remained locked onto her the entire time that she was working on her arm.

"So what do you think doctor, I have potential?" she asked.

She tried to sound amused but she was feeling way too wound up to succeed.

"You have very nice hands."

"You mean good."

"Yeah. Very nice good hands," Kate repeated with a chuckle.

"You sound a little drunk," Tyler observed quietly.

"That would be the morphine. I don't normally take anything, you know... Bandage me up and take me to bed please?"

She gave Tyler a sleepy smile as she spoke, but her eyes told a different story. Tyler wondered if she was aware of how that had sounded, and that every time she looked at her Kate's eyes gave her feelings away. But one look at her incredibly pale face convinced her otherwise.

Although it was difficult, she kept her emotions firmly under control, and carried on with what she was doing. As gently as she could, she wrapped a thick bandage around Kate's arm and secured it in place with several strips of tape. Then she threw her bloody gloves in the trash, thinking that she had had quite enough of the sight of blood for one day.

It was pitch black and very cold as they crossed the camp back to their tent, and Tyler kept a firm grip on Kate, who seemed to struggle a little with walking a straight line.

As always groups of marines were milling around, wide awake, busy with a million little tasks. Still unsettled by the afternoon's events and feeling incredibly restless, Tyler was torn between going out to spend some time with them and staying with Kate. But one look at the injured medic's pale face was enough for her to decide that she should stay put for the time being.

When they got back to their tent Kate sat heavily on her bed and bent forward to undo her laces.

"Let me do that for you," Tyler offered immediately.

She helped to take Kate's boots and trousers off in silence, she helped her to lie down on the bed, and she set a bottle of water within easy reach of her bed.

"Are you warm enough in there?" she asked.

"Toastie…"

As Kate burrowed deeper into her sleeping bag, she reached for Tyler's hand and drew her close.

"Can you stay a bit?" she asked.

"I wasn't going anywhere."

Kate looked unusually small and vulnerable, and Tyler hated seeing her like this. She was reminded of the many friends she had lost to Afghanistan, and again she felt that low threatening buzz of panic deep inside her heart.

"Are you sure you don't want me to get David to have a proper look at you?" she asked again, and she was not surprised when Kate shook her head no.

"And you call me stubborn."

"That's cos you are."

"Oh really?"

"Yes. But I kind of like that about you."

Tyler shook her head and forced a smile, just for Kate. She felt so on edge. She wanted to stay with her, but she had to find something to do or she feared she might literally start to hover around the tent with all the tension of the day.

"How about a bit of music then?" she suggested.

Kate's eyes lit up, and she looked so beautiful all of a sudden it made Tyler's heart ache.

"Yes," she exclaimed. "I haven't even seen your guitar yet."

"Well, it's been a busy few weeks."

Tyler sat on the side of her bed with her guitar cradled in her lap. She smiled as she looked at it.

"This one's been with me through Iraq once, and two tours of Afghanistan," she remarked. "It's taken a few knocks along the way but all it needs is a new set of strings now and then, and it's good to go. So, Ms Sanderson, any special requests for you tonight?"

"Melissa Etheridge," Kate said without hesitation.

"Ha! Good choice…"

Tyler went through the opening chords of several different songs, warming her fingers up. She looked up at Kate, pleased when she saw how attentive she was, yet a little bit uncomfortable at the intensity of her gaze.

"You like this one?" she asked, and she launched into an impeccable version of You Can Sleep While I Drive.

"It's one of my favourites," Kate said, beaming.

"Yeah, me too."

Tyler played for a little while, until she felt the stress of the afternoon begin to fade away, until calm settled inside her heart again. Until she could look at Kate without the thought of her being injured twisting her stomach so hard that she could barely breathe. Music always helped, but tonight it took longer.

"Hey, you're good," Kate said.

Tyler smiled a little. She carried on strumming a slow blues piece, almost absent-mindedly.

"Can I ask you something?" Kate said slowly.

Her voice was heavy with the effects of the morphine, and her eyes were closing. She was so beautiful, Tyler thought, and she was finding it difficult to keep her expression neutral.

"Sure," she said, trying to sound matter of fact.

"You know this afternoon… when it all happened…"

"Yes."

"Were you scared?"

Tyler exhaled slowly. The question brought the tension all back, and she dropped her guitar on her own bed and went to sit back next to Kate. The woman immediately wrapped the fingers of her good hand around her wrist and held on to her. She looked like she was about to cry, and Tyler wondered how far off tears she herself really was.

"Kate..." she murmured.

"Were you?" Kate insisted.

"Yeah," Tyler said simply. "Of course I was scared. We all were, you know."

"But you never look it."

Tyler gave a soft laugh.

"I don't think it would help anyone if I went running off screaming every time something happens," she remarked lightly.

"And you always hide behind a joke, too," Kate observed. "Why is that?"

Tyler shook her head.

"You should get some sleep doc," she observed.

"Please. Talk to me, Ty."

"What do you want me to say?" Tyler's voice was gentle, and a little sad as she added, "I am a platoon commander, Kate. I tell the guys what to do, and I have to believe in what I'm saying, otherwise why would they? It is my job to lead. It is my job to sound calm on the radio. I can't let anyone see what's really going on inside."

Kate watched her in complete silence for a few moments. Tyler grew restless and uncomfortable under her gaze, and she tried to move but Kate kept her there with a single look.

"What is really going on inside, captain?" she asked eventually.

Tyler shook her head in frustration.

"Nothing," she repeated. "I told you, I'm fine."

"No, you're not. And it's okay to let me see, you know..." Kate murmured as her eyes closed.

Once she was sure that she was asleep, Tyler stood up and pulled the hood of the sleeping bag a little tighter around her. She took a deep breath and turned back, feeling a little bit like she did after a contact with the enemy, excited and exhausted all at once.

Kate was very good at doing that to her, she reflected pensively. She was very good at making her feel a lot of things that Tyler did not want to feel again.

She stretched out on her own bed in the dark, thinking that she would just close her eyes for five minutes, and then go out to get something to eat for the both of them. She woke up much later at the sound of crying in the tent, and it only took her half a second to come back to full alertness.

"Kate?" she whispered.

She peered through the darkness and went to sit next to her on the bed.

"Hey, doc. Wake up," she said gently, taking hold of her hand.

At the feel of a hand on her Kate almost catapulted out of bed in shock, and Tyler instinctively caught her in her arms and steadied her.

"Careful," she said, worried that she would rip her stitches open.

"Tyler?" Kate gasped.

"Yeah. Don't worry, everything's fine."

It took a second or two for Kate to realise where she was, and then she held harder on to Tyler. She was shaking uncontrollably.

"Are you okay?" she asked hoarsely.

"Me? Sure, I'm okay."

Kate pulled back a little, her eyes full of tears as she scrutinised her face.

"You were dreaming. I'm fine," Tyler told her again.

"I dreamt that you were shot."

"Just a dream," Tyler said firmly.

Tears welled up in Kate's eyes again and she pulled Tyler hard against her once more, wrapping her arms around her neck.

"It felt so real," she whispered. "You were bleeding. Like Sam this afternoon. And I couldn't do anything to stop it."

This time Tyler was silent.

She tightened her grip on Kate and closed her eyes, taking a deep breath. She tried to force herself to try to think of something else. But frankly, with Kate in her arms, it was too difficult. It had been years since somebody had held her like this, like they meant it. Years since somebody had worried about her, because they really cared. Part of her wanted to run away from it, and another bigger part of her wanted to lose herself in Kate's embrace and never move again.

They stayed like that for what felt like ages, and then Tyler pulled back a little when she felt Kate sigh against her. She turned her head to look at her.

"Are you okay now?" she asked.

She was trying to sound matter of fact about it, but there was just enough light coming through the tent for her to be able to catch the heat in Kate's eyes. Tyler knew what would happen next. She shook her head a little, but she could not make herself look away, not this time.

"Kate. Don't..." she warned.

"Kiss me," Kate said fiercely.

"No."

"Please, Tyler..."

Kate's lips brushed her own, and Tyler made a genuine attempt to pull back, only managing to catch her leg against the bed and fall clumsily back onto it. Kate pressed herself against her, her eyes closing as their mouths met. She kissed her, gently at first, almost as if she wanted to give Tyler a chance to stop. But right this second Tyler was powerless to do so, and the kiss quickly turned harder, demanding.

"Kate, wait," she murmured.

"Shh. That's okay..."

Tyler knew that she had to move and break this up, and things were happening so fast she had to do it pretty quickly too. But whilst her head was thinking one thing, her body was saying quite another. She was struggling to get back in control of herself and of the situation, and then Kate kissed her again, and Tyler was lost.

She felt Kate's fingers travel along the back of her neck and work their way into her hair, and then there was another kiss, this time slow, precise, heavy, as if Kate had decided to make it as hard as possible for Tyler to stop wanting it.

Tyler's heart was racing, and her skin was on fire, incandescent everywhere that Kate touched her. But somewhere inside her heart a tightening occurred, and she started to tense up.

"No... Kate, I... I can't," she murmured.

"It's okay."

"No. Please... Stop."

Tyler finally managed to slide out from under her, and she sat up quickly, not caring that she knocked Kate's open bottle of water onto a bunch of maps as she did so. She took a hard breath, fighting against the overwhelming urge to turn back to her. She glanced at her over her shoulder, noticed the uncertain look in her eyes, the way that she seemed to be about to burst into tears again.

"I can't. I'm sorry," she said.

Her voice was raw with emotion, her heart pounding hard inside her chest.

Seeing the pained look in her eyes, Kate suddenly became aware of how far she had pushed it.

"I'm sorry," she said slowly.

"It's all right. Just forget it."

"This is so unlike me Tyler. I don't know what I was doing..."

Tyler wondered why she suddenly felt like crying.

"Yeah, I think you do," she said, and she was finding it a little too hard to catch her breath. "That's okay, Kate."

She stood up and put some space between them, because she had started to shake so badly she was afraid that Kate would notice and imagine the worst. She was not having a panic attack, and everything was fine.

Yet Kate apologised again.

"Don't worry," Tyler told her, more firmly this time. "You didn't do anything wrong, it's me. I just... I'm not..." She struggled with the words, and finally gave up. "Just don't worry about it. I promise you it's fine."

She grabbed her jacket and rifle, and she escaped out into the freezing night, not giving Kate a chance to say anything else.

Not sure where to go, but needing to spend some time on her own, Tyler headed straight toward the back of the shower block. She found a spot in darkness away from prying eyes, and she sat down against the wall, pretty much exactly where Collins had sat the previous night. She dropped her rifle by her side, brought her knees up, and wrapped her arms around them. She stared into the darkness ahead, and shivered in the cold wind as she tried to make sense of what had just happened.

As far as Kate's behaviour was concerned, she blamed it on the morphine. And on getting shot, obviously. Anyone would have needed to blow off some steam after that. Tyler was the only other woman around, so there.

As for her own reaction to Kate, Tyler did not have to dig very deep to understand the mechanics of it, and it scared the hell out of her. Kate was a few years older; she was a highly intelligent, very capable woman. She was beautiful, caring and gentle. Just like Helen had been, at least in the beginning.

And Tyler had zero defence against that.

She pulled the hood of her jacket lower down over her head and shut her eyes tight. She tried to picture Helen in her mind. She tried to remember her voice, her laughter, her smile. But as always all she could remember of her lover was the expression in her eyes on the morning that she had died.

Before the old panic had a chance to grab hold of her, Tyler stood up and punched the make-shift wooden wall behind her with all her strength, so hard it brought tears to her eyes. Then she quickly walked over to Collins' tent, knowing he was the only person she could turn to in that particular moment.

She found him sat comfortably on his bed, alone, cleaning his weapon. He knew as soon as she walked in that something was not right with her. She spoke before he had a chance to ask.

"Ben, let's go do some phys," Tyler announced.

Her voice was tight and unusually strained, and even though this was the last thing in the world he wanted to do right now, he just nodded and grabbed his running shoes.

"You need a beasting, buddy?"

"Yeah."

She would not look him in the eye, and there were times with Tyler when he knew to remain silent and just go with the flow.

"Let's go," he simply said.

They were outside working out for just under an hour, and Tyler ended up feeling like her arms and legs would fall off, but she also knew that there would be no panic attacks now, just sore muscles, and hopefully, much needed sleep.

She crept back into her tent just after one in the morning and found Kate fast asleep, wrapped up deep in her sleeping bag, looking peaceful. There was a shiny bar of Dairy Milk waiting for her on her own bed, and a little note that simply said "Sorry! X." right next to it.

Tyler smiled in spite of herself.

She stood there for a little while, feeling a lot calmer now. She looked down at Kate thoughtfully, feeling like she had known her for years rather than just the few weeks they had actually spent together.

Without thinking, she sat down by the side of her bed and rested her arm on it. She closed her eyes.

"Tyler."

Tyler's head snapped up in surprise. She had dozed off for a few minutes, and now Kate was looking at her with a very worried look in her eyes. This time Tyler found it hard to shake the sleep out of her mind.

"Sorry," she muttered. "Tired…"

She got to her feet with difficulty and she started to move away, but Kate stopped her with a single look.

"Tyler, would you please come lie down with me?" she murmured.

Tyler opened her mouth to speak, but no words came out. Seeing the conflict and the confusion shining in her normally clear grey eyes, Kate simply reached out for her.

"Just please come here."

Tyler bit her lower lip and hesitated. Then, tired of fighting, she finally gave in. She kicked her boots off, threw her jacket across the tent, and stretched out beside Kate. Her right hand was throbbing where she had hit the wall, and she made sure that it remained well out of sight. Kate put her arms around her and pulled her close. Tyler did not resist this time.

"You're freezing," Kate said gently.

She threw a blanket over her and rubbed her hands slowly over her back.

"Is this okay?"

"Yeah... Thanks."

Kate kissed the top of her head.

"No problem. Go back to sleep."

"I'm sorry about before," Tyler mumbled.

"Don't be. I jumped on you. I'm the one who should apologise."

"Morphine talking."

Kate was about to argue that no, it had nothing to do with the morphine, but she remained silent. She did not want to lose Tyler right now, and she had a feeling it would not take much for her to run. Kate was just grateful for the opportunity to be close. Nothing else.

After a couple of minutes she felt Tyler's breathing deepen, and her body went limp in her arms. Exhausted, but feeling better than she had in months, Kate burrowed deeper against her, and after a moment she drifted off too.

Chapter Nine

Kate woke up at dawn, immediately reached for Tyler, and realised that she was alone. Shivering, she looked across to the other bed, but Tyler was not in the tent. It was just after five in the morning, still dark outside.

As she slowly remembered the events of the previous day, Kate shook her head in dismay. She could not quite believe what she had done. It had been stupid, it was unforgiveable, and she hoped that Tyler would understand. They would need to talk.

Tyler walked in a minute later. Her hair was wet and her eyes were bright and free of the shadows of the night before. She was wearing her usual combats and a thick winter jacket, and she was armed with a toothbrush instead of her rifle. She looked beautiful, and just a little bit unsure. She had gone out early, needing to clear her head before she saw Kate again.

The previous night had been equal measures hard and wonderful for her. She had run away when Kate had wanted her, and yet falling asleep in her arms later had been the most incredible thing in the world.

"Morning doc," she said briskly. "How are you? How is your arm?"

Kate smiled a little.

"It's fine. Your stitches have held up beautifully. Are you okay?"

Tyler nodded, and she observed Kate in silence for a second. Then she shoved her hands into her pockets and gave a thoughtful shrug.

"Well," she reflected, "I guess that's a result, considering…"

"Considering the session last night?" Kate said bluntly.

Tyler gave a soft chuckle. She was smiling, and she could not stop no matter how much she tried. Kate was all wrapped up in her sleeping bag, her hair was tousled with sleep, and her eyes were shining with a mixture of embarrassment and tenderness. It was all Tyler could do not to go to her and start all over again. But then she felt her bruised hand rub against the inside of her pocket, and a shadow crossed her face briefly.

Kate saw this and raised a concerned eyebrow.

"Hey, I really am sorry. You forgive me?"

Tyler shook her head.

"Nothing to forgive, doc. No drama."

She held up the Dairy Milk, tore off the wrapper and offered the first bite to Kate.

"Just keep you away from the morphine next time," she said with a smile.

Again, Kate decided to let that slide.

"Chocolate at breakfast?" she questioned instead.

"Yeah, don't you know that's how officers do it?"

With a grin, Kate tore a chunk off and handed it back to Tyler.

"Very decadent. I like it."

She noticed how quickly Tyler averted her gaze when she got up and hunted for her trousers. Not wanting to make it any harder for her, she got into her combats as quickly as she could and pulled on her boots. It was obvious that Tyler was attracted to her too, and she really thought that they should have a chat. But she would take her cue from the officer, and it was obvious that she was in no hurry to have it.

"It's freezing," she said, glancing outside and shivering visibly.

"Here, put this on."

Tyler threw her one of her thermal tops, and she glanced at her watch.

"We should check your arm again, just in case," she said.

"Okay?"

Kate heard the tension in her voice, and saw it reflected in her eyes. This was unusual with Tyler, and she gazed at her in wonder.

"Yes. We can do that in a bit," she said. "Everything all right with you?"

"Yes, fine."

Tyler nodded and turned her back on her. She started to check her patrol kit. She shoved extra magazines into her Bergen, dropped one on the floor and swore under her breath.

Kate hesitated but then decided to ask again.

"Are you sure?" she said. "You sound nervous, and it's not like you. If you want to talk..."

Tyler tightened the straps on her rucksack, seeming to brace herself before she turned around and looked at Kate.

"Okay, well. The thing is I don't want you to go out on patrol with us today," she said finally.

Kate was taken aback by the response. She had expected a lot of things, but definitely not this. She raised her eyebrows, her eyes wide.

"What? Why not?" she exclaimed.

"Because you got shot yesterday," Tyler reminded her gently.

"Oh, come on!"

Tyler had not expected this to go down well anyway, so she just ploughed on with what she had to say.

"I'm only telling you the exact same thing I would tell any of my guys, Kate. Even if it was Ben, the best in my troop, I would not let him go. You've had a rough night, and you need to be one hundred percent fit out there. You know that."

Kate snorted loudly.

"Oh, really? And how many hours of sleep did you get last night, captain?" she argued. "And what about your..."

She stopped before she mentioned the panic attack. She knew it would have been going too far. Tyler's expression did not change,

98

but Kate knew that she understood.

"Hey, this is not personal," Tyler said softly.

Kate stood her ground in front of her, hands on her hips, having forgotten all about how cold it was in the tent. Her eyes were flashing and her cheeks were burning. Tyler looked at her, and she knew for sure that Kate had absolutely no idea how beautiful she looked at that very moment, and how badly Tyler wanted to kiss her. She turned away and got busy with her gear again.

"Does this have anything to do with what happened between us last night?"

"No. Absolutely not."

Kate stared deep into Tyler's eyes, looking for the truth she knew would be there. When the corner of her mouth twitched, and a half smile flickered in her eyes, she thought that she had found it.

"Tyler," she demanded. "Please be honest with me."

"I mean it," Tyler said quietly. "Nothing to do with yesterday."

"What then?"

"Just what I said."

"But..."

"Listen, Kate, you are a doctor first, not a soldier. It's my job to make sure that you stay safe."

"No. I am a soldier and a doctor in equal parts. And maybe you could let me decide for myself."

Tyler raised an eyebrow.

"What would you do if it was me?" she asked boldly.

This did stop Kate in her tracks. She remembered how good it had felt to hold Tyler in her arms. How strong and beautiful she was, and yet how fragile she could be as well when her emotions became just that little bit too much for her. She was not as unbreakable as she thought she was, and Kate was terrified that something would happen to her.

She rolled her shoulders and shook her head a little, then attempted a joke.

"I would lock you up in a cell in Alcatraz so I can know you're safe," she said.

Tyler gave a silent smile.

Kate sighed and looked down at her injured arm, feeling the stitches sting a little under her bandage. She did feel quite a bit under the weather, and she knew she was running a fever.

"Okay," she said slowly. "Okay, you win."

"It's not about winning or losing, doc, it's about being safe."

"I know."

Tyler shouldered her rucksack, feeling reluctant to leave.

"Go back to bed, okay? I'll ask Ben to check in on you in a bit."

"He's not going out? How come?"

"Scheduled R&R."

"Right. And Tyler?"

"Yes?"

"Thanks. And be careful out there, okay?"

Tyler flashed a bright smile and saluted briefly.

"Always."

The patrol lasted six hours, and for the first time in a long while not a single shot was fired. Maybe it was the weather, which had definitely taken a turn for the worst. Whatever it was, Tyler walked back into Cobel with a smile on her face, tired, but happy to be able to bring everybody back safe and sound. She stopped by the Ops room for a quick debrief with Major Cox, and then headed straight back to her tent.

She found Kate fast asleep, all cocooned inside her sleeping bag and wearing her USMC hoody for extra warmth. Careful not to make any noise, she grabbed a change of clothes and headed for the showers, popping in to see Collins along the way.

He was stretched out on his bed reading a magazine, and smiled when he saw her.

"Hey boss. How's it going?"

"Great, thanks."

"Patrol go okay?"

"Perfect. So did you keep an eye on Kate today?"

Collins nodded, smiling a little at Tyler's impatient tone.

"Yeah, I did. Not that she was awake much. Think the day off would have done her a world of good."

"Okay. Thanks for looking after her."

She was about to walk back out when Collins sat up and gestured for her to wait.

"She was worried about you," he said, watching her.

Tyler frowned.

"What do you mean? Why?"

His expression softened and he resisted rolling his eyes.

"Do I really have to spell it out for you, Tyler," he said patiently.

He called her boss most of the times, especially when on tour. But he was her friend, first and foremost, and this was definitely one of these times.

"You know for someone so intelligent, sometimes you're a bit slow on the uptake."

Tyler went still and simply looked at him.

He shrugged.

"Come on, it's obvious she cares about you. And she got a bit upset earlier on, so I'm just making sure everything's okay between you guys."

Tyler felt herself grow hot at his words, and her heart tightened.

"Of course... We're fine. What happened?"

"She was cold, so I grabbed your sweater and gave it to her. And she burst into tears. Wouldn't tell me why, gave me some bullshit about not reacting well to pain killers. You guys had a fight?"

"No," Tyler protested.

"You sure?"

"Yes," she snapped.

Collins studied her for a few seconds, knowing there was something more going on. But then he just touched her arm briefly.

"Ah well, don't worry then. Probably just feeling a little rough after yesterday."

"Yeah," Tyler muttered. "Probably."

"Probably could do with a hug, too," he added, and when Tyler met his gaze he stared straight back at her. "And not one from me, if you see what I mean. Tyler, I told you before, I think this is a chance for you to..."

Tyler gave a sharp nod, afraid of what he might say next.

"Yeah. I'll see you later."

"Don't rush it."

"I won't. And Ben?"

"Yeah?"

Tyler gave him a heartfelt smile.

"Thanks."

Tyler walked back to the tent, just needing to get back to Kate as quickly as possible. She did not give herself any time, to think, stall or remind herself again why Kate was a bad idea. She zipped the canvas door shut behind her, kicked her boots off, and climbed into bed next to her.

"Ty?" Kate mumbled, still half asleep.

"Who else are you expecting?" Tyler murmured close to her ear.

She felt Kate chuckle, and she wrapped her arms more tightly around her. With the sound of Kate's soft laugh against her ear, Tyler felt her defences slip and tension melt away.

She exhaled slowly.

"So. How did you enjoy spending the day with my sidekick?" she asked.

"I think I fell asleep on him rather a lot."

"Hmm. He did mention that, yes."

Kate twisted round until she could look Tyler in the eye.

"I think it may have been a good idea to give me the day off today," she said.

"Wow. Are you saying I was right?"

"Maybe."

Tyler smiled.

"Cool," she said. "I'll take maybe."

"Your turn."

"Yes?"

"What are you doing in my bed, captain?" Kate asked gently.

Tyler kept smiling but her eyes grew a little bit darker.

"Giving you a hug," she said.

"Hey, that's nice," Kate murmured. "What else you got?"

Tyler was silent, and Kate twisted until she was facing her. Tyler had that look on her face, conflicted, torn. Her eyes were on Kate, and yet Kate could tell that part of her was miles away, lost in memories again. Gently, she reached up and cradled Tyler's jaw in her hand. She waited until Tyler focused on her again, and she smiled.

"It's okay, you know..." she said.

"What is?"

"This. Being together. Being close."

Tyler's left hand strayed inside her sleeping bag and came to rest on her naked thigh.

Kate closed her eyes, feeling heat spread between her legs. She shifted a little, and Tyler's hand drifted further down, to her knee, coming back up the inside of her thigh. Kate moved her legs apart a little and sighed.

"Keep going captain," she whispered.

Tyler buried her face in her hair and took a trembling breath. Her hand moved higher, and as Kate struggled not to whimper out loud she paused.

"Ah, Kate... I don't know what I'm doing here," she whispered.

"Of course you do."

"Are you sure?" Tyler insisted. "This is nuts."

Her voice was low, husky. There was no denying the desire in her tone, nor the hesitation.

"I'm sure."

"This is all I can give you, Kate," Tyler murmured softly against her ear. "Just tonight... How can it be okay when I can't even..."

Kate reached up and clasped the back of her neck, bringing her down for a long, torrid kiss. Tyler groaned. Now she was lost.

"Stop talking," Kate murmured.

She kissed Tyler again, more softly this time. She knew the woman needed her to be gentle. She felt it in the way she trembled in her arms, and when she touched her face she felt her tears.

"Why are you crying?" she asked tenderly.

"I'm not," Tyler said.

Kate stifled a cry as she apparently cast her doubts aside, and once more let her fingers play over her skin. She tried to keep her eyes open. She wanted to give back, but Tyler's touch was so expertly tender she could do nothing but drift.

"It's okay. Just let go," Tyler whispered in her ear.

She kissed the side of her neck, her eyelids, her lips. Now Kate was lost.

Chapter Ten

Almost a day later, in the middle of a muddy field, she tensed as Tyler's voice came through on the team radio.

"Go firm, guys."

Every marine on the line stopped. Most dropped a knee down, each of them focusing on their surroundings, listening, watching. The area was amazingly quiet.

Earlier on there had been people walking around, kids running up to them, shaking hands, smiles all around. Now it was deathly quiet. Kate knew from past experience that it was a bad sign. Either they were about to get shot at, or this was a mined area. Either way, she was feeling nervous.

"Got any I-Comm?"

Tyler asked the usual question over the radio.

Kate exhaled slowly, turning her head a little until she could see her. There was something about Tyler's voice, speaking right against her ear, that never failed to start her heart beat a little faster. She knew now that it would not give her any real clue as to Tyler's true state of mind, but it was a reassurance nonetheless. And as she thought of their time together the previous night she immediately wanted to smile.

"Got I-Comm."

Collins' voice burst through a wall of static, bringing her back to now.

"Usual shit. Kill the infidels, make em bleed, blah blah blah…"

"Getting boring."

"Yeah boss."

"Okay then, let's push on. Everybody cover your arcs."

Kate stood up again. She took a sip of water, tightened her grip on her rifle, started forward. There were some trees up ahead and they were only a mile away from camp. Earlier on that morning they had stopped at a village and she and Tyler had managed to see and speak to some of the women. Another major achievement. Her arm ached but not too much. She allowed herself to think about home.

Then Collins came on the net again.

"Got a guy approaching from the North. He's carrying something."

"Go firm," Tyler ordered again immediately.

She looked in that direction and spotted the individual straight away. He was wearing a white dish dash, looked to be about forty years old. He was smiling, and gesturing for the soldiers to come to him. After a couple of seconds he started approaching them, and stopped again when he was within shouting distance. People in the area knew not to run at soldiers, and not to rush them either.

"What's he saying?" Tyler asked impatiently.

Collins was a trained interpreter. He made his way slowly to the newcomer, and Tyler saw the man open the bundle he was carrying and show it to him.

"He's got a dead baby," Collins relayed via the radio. "On his way to the cemetery. Guy's crying."

"Stay put, I'm coming over," Tyler instructed.

She got to her feet and made her way to Collins and the villager. The man did not pay much attention to her, and he spoke to Collins and Collins only.

Tyler did not feel she had a lot of patience in her this morning, and she was bothered by his attitude. There was something about the man she did not like, but she could not quite put her finger on it.

"What's he saying?" she asked again, finally managing to make eye contact with him, if only for a couple of seconds.

"Wants to know if you're the commander," Collins translated. "I told him yes. He is happy."

"Why's he happy about that? Ask him what happened to the baby."

The man lifted the bundle toward Tyler as if he wanted her to take it, but she did not move an inch.

"He says the baby got sick in the night and died."

"Just like that?"

Collins shrugged.

"Apparently, yeah."

"Tell him we have a medic with us. We can help the people in the village if they have any other sick kids."

Kate was not close enough to understand every word of what was being said, but she got the gist of it and could clearly see that the man was upset. He spoke animatedly to Tyler and Collins. Collins was listening intently. Tyler stood by the side of him, nodding from time to time. She looked tense, but Kate gave a soft smile as she watched her. She saw Tyler say something to the Afghan, and glance back to where Kate stood, flashing her a quick private smile when she caught her eyes on her. She held her gaze, took a few steps back toward her, and Kate started to do the same.

And then there was a single shout, and all hell broke loose.

When it happened, the force of the explosion threw Kate to the ground and took her breath away. All sounds faded, and everything appeared to sink into slow motion. She sat up slowly, feeling numb. When she looked around her, she realised that she could no longer see anybody else through all the dust hanging in the air. She frowned and shook her head a little, unsure what had just happened.

Then there were shouts on the radio, and everything rushed back into focus, much, much too fast. She scrambled back up to her feet. She turned around, and with her head and her heart pounding, she started to run toward the smoke. Her hearing was coming back and she was suddenly aware of several voices shouting for her.

At the back of her mind Kate was aware that Tyler's voice had not come on the radio, although somebody was asking for an evac Chinook. Her temper picked up as she ran. They had no sit rep yet, and she would be the one to issue a casualty report back to base and request a Chinook pickup, if required. What did they know that she had not come across yet?

Then she stumbled over something on the ground and went flying. When she looked back, she froze.

"Jesus..." she murmured, appalled at what she saw.

It was Collins, and yet it was not. The tall, friendly marine's legs had been blown off. His right arm was gone. His face was burnt so badly he was barely recognizable.

Kate took all this in and she had to stop for a second. She felt sick, dizzy. She wanted to scream. She leaned forward, hands on her knees, and forced herself to breathe. Long stretches of blackness flew in front of her eyes.

She fought them hard.

She glanced back at Collins, only once, and said a silent prayer for him. Then she forced herself to push on. She came across a young marine next, covered in blood. She grabbed his hands to stop him from shaking so much.

"Look at me," she said loudly. "Look at me! Hey! Are you hurt?"

He shook his head, in a daze.

"No. I'm okay. It's his... Collins. His blood... Shit..."

"Take your time. Breathe."

He shook his head, gestured that he was all right.

"That guy blew himself up!" he said loudly, his voice breaking a little as he spoke. "I saw him grab Collins just before he detonated himself. Fucking suicide bomber!"

Kate stood up once more and looked around her, fear twisting her stomach.

"Tyler!" she shouted. "Ty!"

There was more than a hint of desperation in her voice. Tyler had been too close to Collins to have escaped getting hurt. Kate knew this. At least the rational part of her brain did. But her soul would not accept it. She remembered Tyler that very morning, smiling at her in the tent. She remembered the taste of her mouth and the feel of her skin. Tyler would be okay. She had to be, there was no other way. Kate felt panic rise inside her chest once more. Where the hell was she?

"Tyler!" she yelled, her voice breaking.

Then she spotted a small group of soldiers gesturing toward her. She sprinted to them, and at last she knew. Tyler was lying on the ground in the middle of the group.

She was not moving.

Kate dropped to her knees next to her and immediately searched for a pulse. Her fingers were shaking almost uncontrollably, but she steadied herself and pushed her fingers against the side of Tyler's neck, closing her eyes as she did so. She had to push hard in order to feel a heartbeat, and she almost cried in relief when she felt it. Tyler was alive.

"Guys, I need some space," she told the marines gathered around them. "Back off, please!"

They moved quickly and in silence, their faces grave.

Tyler had lost her helmet in the explosion. Her fatigues were ripped in places and her hair was dark with blood, her face deathly pale. When Kate saw the state of her left leg it knocked the breath out of her once more. Unable to help herself, she bent over her and framed her face in her hands.

"Tyler, can you hear me?" she called. "Please open your eyes. Tyler!"

Lenster came to kneel next to her.

"I've got medic training, can I help?" he asked.

He swore under his breath when he saw Tyler's leg.

Kate barely glanced at him as she yanked an IV line and several shots of morphine out of her Bergen.

"Can you get a line into her?" she asked.

"Sure."

"Okay. Quick as you can."

Lenster set to work, and Kate bent over Tyler's leg, frowning in concentration. She jumped in fright when Tyler grabbed her arm and pulled her back, hard enough to make her lose her balance.

"Tyler, it's me," Kate said quickly, catching the disorientation in her eyes.

"Chinook is on the way boss," Lenster said loudly. "We're getting an Apache to clean up the unwanted first."

Tyler stared at him in disbelief, then at the needle in her arm, and she tried to raise herself up on one elbow.

"What... what are you doing?" she protested.

She turned to Kate, and her eyes travelled over her body armour before coming to rest on her face.

She blinked furiously.

"Kate. Are you injured?" she gasped.

"No, I'm fine."

"You're covered in blood!"

Kate forced a reassuring smile. She grabbed bandages from her bag, working quickly, not pausing to talk for long.

"It's not mine, Tyler," she said. "Try to relax, okay?"

"Lenster, help me get up," Tyler snapped angrily. "Did we get hit? I don't..."

She stopped abruptly and stared at her leg. Kate felt her tremble.

She wanted to cry when she spotted the look on Tyler's face, recognising frustration, anger, and a huge amount of fear all wrapped into one. She wished she could have hugged her then and reassured them both that she was going to be okay. But there was no time for that, and she was not going to start lying to her now.

So she kept her focus and started to cut through the remains of her trousers. She was working as quickly as she could, concerned that

Tyler was losing a lot of blood. There was so much of it that it was hard even for Kate to see exactly the full extent of the damage.

"How are you doing?" she asked. "Talk to me."

Tyler did not reply. It took her a few seconds to make sense of what she was seeing, because it was so unexpected to see it on herself, and because she still felt dizzy from the shock of the explosion. She had seen soldiers wounded before, gunshot wounds and limbs torn apart by IEDs, grenades and shrapnel. But for a moment she struggled to link the sight of her shattered leg to her own self. Most of the bone below her knee was gone, and it looked like only a single tendon still connected her foot to her leg.

She gritted her teeth as shock and pain hit her like a freight train.

"Fuck," she muttered.

Another platoon from the camp had arrived by now, and a big group of marines were busy establishing a safe landing zone for the evac helicopter. Anybody wanting to take a shot at them had better be prepared to die in the process. At least it might be relatively safe doing the extraction, Kate reflected.

She realised that Tyler was going to leave, and she clenched her teeth.

"Get me on the radio," Tyler ordered Lenster.

He quickly gave it to her, and Tyler fought to control her breathing as she got back on the net.

"Is everybody okay?" she asked, and Kate threw her a sharp glance. She was shaking like a leaf.

A chaos of voices came back over the net. A lot of swearing and anger came through. And confirmations that an Apache was about to do very bad things to a bunch of confirmed Taliban hiding in a nearby wood. Nobody was going to intercept the rescue helicopter.

Tyler dropped the radio and sank a little lower.

"I'm not leaving," she said through gritted teeth.

"Listen…"

"No. I'm not going."

Her voice was hard but the trembling was getting worse.

"Fuck!" she repeated, and Kate was worried that this was going downhill way too fast.

She took Tyler's face in both her hands and touched her lips with hers. She did not give a damn who was around anymore, this was far too important.

"Listen to me," she said quietly. "I need you to calm down, okay? Stay still and let me do my job."

Pain blazed through Tyler's eyes and she struggled to speak.

"I need... Ben. Where's Ben?"

Kate looked up and her eyes met Lenster's.

The marine's jaw clenched and he looked like he was about to be sick.

"Kate?" Tyler insisted. "Is he okay?"

Kate rested her fingers against her cheek and lowered her voice.

"No. He's not," she murmured.

"What?"

"I'm sorry Ty. Ben is gone. Now please lie down."

She averted her eyes and turned once more to Tyler's leg.

Kate felt on the verge of despair as she applied fresh compresses against the side of it, aware that she was fighting a losing battle. There was too much blood, the injury was too severe to be treated in the middle of a dirty field, and she felt both angry and scared at the same time as she tightened the tourniquet on Tyler's leg and glanced over her shoulder.

"ETA on that Chinook?" she yelled back.

She struggled not to swear, knowing it would not help, knowing she had to keep calm for Tyler's sake.

"Two minutes, doc."

"Kate," Tyler said weakly. "You sure about Ben?"

Kate winced involuntarily.

"I'm sure. I'm sorry," she repeated.

Tyler seemed to give up then. She did lie down finally, and after a couple of seconds she brought her arms up and crossed them in front of her face. She started to sob silently.

Kate wrapped her fingers around her wrist and pulled her arm back.

"Don't do this now," she ordered. "Please. Don't give in. I need you to stay awake and keep talking to me."

But Tyler was struggling to keep her eyes open by now. She was getting worse with every passing second, and Kate knew that they were running out of time.

"Open your eyes, damn it!" she shouted.

"They'll cut my leg off... in Bastion..."

This made Kate feel a little as if someone had just punched her in the stomach. The way that Tyler stated the obvious, with so little emotion, as if she were not talking about her own self. Kate wanted to tell her no, that she would be okay, but she knew that Tyler would be lucky if she managed to keep her knee.

"Hey, Ty, tell me about the beach at home," she said instead.

She looked up as the Chinook started approaching, low and fast over the frozen fields. Tyler was leaving. They did not have much time now.

She squeezed her hand, hard.

"Look at me," she urged.

Tyler's eyes remained closed, and Kate bent even closer to her.

"You have to hold on," she implored. "You hear me? Tyler!"

Tyler finally opened her eyes, and struggled to speak.

"Be careful," she murmured.

"Always."

"I'm sorry, Kate..."

"Shhh. You've got nothing to be sorry about."

Kate took a hard breath. She lay her hand over Tyler's forehead, letting her fingers drift to her cheek, feeling the skin burning underneath.

"You're going to be okay," she said, as firmly as her own fear allowed her to.

Out of the corner of her eye she spotted the evac Chinook about to land. She lay on top of Tyler to protect her from the down blast, and in the next second they got drenched in wet mud lifted from the powerful blades. Tyler held on to her, and Kate bit her lip when she felt how badly she was shaking.

"It's okay, it's okay," she kept on repeating.

She brushed her eyes before Tyler could see that she was crying, and she looked down at her.

"Nearly there, darling," she said with an encouraging smile. "You're going home, you're going to be okay."

"No. Stay with me," Tyler murmured.

Kate looked up as the army medics arrived on scene. Reluctantly, she moved away from her injured friend.

"What's her status?" one of them asked as they moved her onto a stretcher.

"Cat B," Kate replied, fighting tears.

They were fastening the straps on the stretcher, covering her with an emergency blanket.

"BP's plunging," his colleague announced. "We need to go now."

Kate ran with them back to the helicopter. She stumbled a couple of times, feeling weak and out of breath. She was beginning to lose control and she knew it.

As the medics ran up the ramp and lowered the stretcher inside the helicopter, Kate glanced at Tyler and caught her eyes on her. She was struggling to remain conscious and her face was ashen, but her eyes were open. Kate bent down to her and put her mouth to her ear. The sound of the Chinook was deafening, and she shouted so that she could be certain that Tyler would hear her.

"You're doing great," she said breathlessly. "Keep fighting. I will come and find you. I promise."

Tyler shook her head but her eyes were closing again in spite of herself. The helicopter shuddered, ready to lift. One of the medics applied an oxygen mask to her face and turned to Kate.

"We gotta go, are you going or staying?" he yelled.

"Going."

Kate allowed herself to look back at Tyler just once. She touched her cheek, squeezed her hand one last time, and then she jumped out of the helicopter and ran back to the troops.

Chapter Eleven

When Tyler came to she had absolutely no idea where she was, although she knew instinctively that this was not a place she wanted to be. The air around her was strange, congested with the smells of blood, antiseptic, and something else that she could not place. The infirmary at Cobel? It was hot, dark and stuffy. It felt like the middle of the night, and she tried in vain to identify where she was and remember how she had got there. It was hard to think. Her brain felt sluggish and heavy, and every bit of her body hurt, even more than the night after her last Ironman.

It was quite impossible to stay awake much longer, and she drifted off again.

Just over a day later, she started to awaken at the feel of a cool hand on her forehead. After a while she recognised the sound of a woman's voice, very faint.

That got her attention.

"Kate…" she murmured.

Her throat was dry. The headache was worse than before, and she struggled to open her eyes.

"Kate," she said again, louder this time.

"Captain Jackson?"

Tyler opened her eyes and blinked. Damn it was bright in this room. She blew air out loudly and tried to adjust her vision.

"Captain?"

The woman standing next to the bed came into focus. She had short spiky red hair and bright green eyes. She wore a uniform and sergeant stripes under her white coat. Not Kate.

Tyler narrowed her eyes at her.

"Hey there," the woman said loudly. "Do you know where you are, captain? Do you remember what happened?"

Tyler shook her head a little and the simple fact of doing so made her feel like someone had planted an axe right in between her eyes. She closed them again and exhaled slowly. Now that she knew the woman was not Kate, she was not interested in talking to her, and all she wanted to do was sink back into sleep. The light hurt her eyes and she longed for darkness, but the sergeant would have none of it.

"Can you tell me your name, captain?"

"Jackson," Tyler muttered.

"First name?"

"Tyler."

"That's good. I'm Sergeant O'Connor. Can you open your eyes for me? Do you know where you are?"

"Hospital. I don't know where I am."

The second Tyler said that it hit her. Everything came flooding back all at once, and she sat bolt upright, ripping the IV line out of her arm, hard enough to start it bleeding.

"Whoa, take it easy," the doctor exclaimed.

She gripped Tyler's wrist and immediately applied a compress against her arm.

"Calm down. You're safe here."

Tyler's heart was racing.

She glanced at the syringe in the woman's hand.

"I don't need that," she said.

"It's just morphine. Believe me, it will help."

"No. I don't want drugs," Tyler argued loudly, and her head was clearing at the speed of light, memories getting sharper as adrenaline rushed through her.

"Okay, just let me know when you change your mind."

"I won't. Where am I?"

The doctor sank her hands in the pockets of her white coat and

117

gazed at her patiently.

"How are you feeling?" she asked.

"I just remembered... what happened yesterday. Where am I, is this Bastion?"

"Actually, that was just over three days ago now. You've been out a while."

Three days? Tyler let that sink in, her mind working overdrive to piece the bits back together.

"What's your normal resting heart rate?"

"Forty-eight."

O'Connor nodded in appreciation, and she wrapped her fingers around Tyler's wrist. She glanced at her watch, then shot a concerned look at her patient.

"You're at ninety three right now."

"That's because I don't know what the hell is going on!" Tyler shouted.

"Okay. Calm down..."

"No! Don't touch me!"

Tyler rolled over and took a wild swing in the general direction of the doctor's head.

Then she vaguely heard the woman call for help, and almost immediately someone else was in there with them. She felt someone hold her down, and something very cold pressed against her face, and then silent darkness flooded her mind once more and dragged her down into unconsciousness.

When she opened her eyes again she found O'Connor standing by the side of her bed, looking wary. Tyler spotted the cut on her lower lip, and she sighed.

"Ha. Did I do this?" she asked.

"Don't worry about it.

"Well. I'm very sorry."

O'Connor flashed her a genuine smile.

"Really, captain. It's nothing, don't worry."

"Is this Bastion?" Tyler asked tiredly.

"Yes."

"Then I don't want drugs."

"Okay, that's fine."

"Where's my weapon?"

"You're on your way out of here, captain," O'Connor explained. "No weapons allowed on the plane."

Tyler stared at her, working to wrap her head around this novel bit of news. Then she looked down and narrowed her eyes at the unfamiliar shape of her legs under the thin hospital cover.

The doctor followed her gaze.

"Do you remember what happened?" she said quietly.

Tyler barely heard her. All of a sudden she was back in the field after the explosion. She stared into space and felt herself grow rigid as she remembered what her leg had looked like. She remembered the medic on the helicopter telling her to stay with him, that she had to stay awake. Voices swirling around her as she kept drifting in and out of consciousness, and then everything accelerating as a man in scrubs bent over her leg and shook his head. She remembered the mask against her face and the sweet smell of anaesthetic, and surrendering to it because she could no longer fight it, knowing what they were going to do.

Tyler gave a tense shake of the head. It was a shock to see that a big part of her left leg was no longer there.

"Captain Jackson."

Tyler looked up at the doctor at the same time that she realised she was crying. She brushed the tears away, angry with herself for losing control so easily.

"It's okay," the doctor said gently. "Do you want to tell me about it?"

Tyler swallowed, still staring at her leg.

"Suicide bomber," she said slowly.

"Where were you at the time?"

"Out on patrol..."

She started to shake.

"Sorry," she murmured.

"It's okay. Just let it go."

"Why am I shaking like this?"

"Shock. That's pretty normal, don't worry."

Tyler fought to control the shaking and failed.

"My leg... looked pretty bad after the explosion," she said, looking up at the doctor. "I didn't think you'd be able to save it, but I was hoping you could at least save my knee..."

She bit her lower lip and went quiet. She had been hoping against all hope that there was something they would be able to do to save her leg. And the thought that they would take it off above the knee had never even entered her mind.

O'Connor gave her a gentle smile and nodded.

"I know," she said. "The surgeons did everything they could, but the damage was too extensive, and there was a risk of infection. They had to cut just above the knee. This being said, you should have no complications with it, so long as you don't rush your rehab."

Tyler pretty much ignored that last comment.

"When can I get a prosthetic?" she asked. "I need to be walking."

"We're flying you out to the UK, and you are going straight to Staunton Forest. You can start your rehab over there pretty much straight away."

This was enough to distract Tyler from her leg for a second.

"England?" she repeated.

"Yes. Is that a problem? You'll need to speak to your command if you'd like to go back to the US first..."

"No, England's perfect," Tyler interrupted. "I just..."

She breathed deeply and felt herself relax a little. Any connection to Kate was a boost of morale at the minute.

"England's great, thanks," she said.

"We aim to please. I'll go and check on timings for you, be still and wait for me, okay?"

Alone once more, Tyler took a deep breath and slowly removed the cover off her legs. Her left thigh was heavily bandaged, and she was grateful for that. She realised as she stared down that she had not been quite ready to look at the injury yet, and the white bandage covered it completely and made it easier to come to terms with. It looked neat and clean. Her hands shook a little still, but she took several deep breaths and remained firmly in control. It would be okay. She would get a prosthetic and she would still be able to run. She would still be able to walk. It was all that mattered.

She lay back on the bed and stared at the ceiling, frustration taking hold as she thought of her platoon and the marines she had left behind.

Collins.

Her mind drifted back to their meeting with the Afghan. She remembered he had asked if she was the boss, and he was happy when Collins said that she was. Tyler remembered the little grin on his face. She knew now why he had been smiling. He knew he was going to blow them both up and he was delighted the boss was going to be on his list of victims. She understood now why she had felt so unnerved during the brief conversation. She had been aware that something was not right, but at the time she thought that the danger would come from an attack from an enemy they had not spotted yet.

She had had no idea the enemy was standing right in front of her.

"Ben…" she murmured.

Dead.

She turned the words around in her head, whispered her friend's name again, remembered him. Dead. This did not feel real either, and she struggled to keep her panic in check.

When she thought about Kate, stuck at Cobel on her own, it

nearly sent her over the edge.

Her heart jumped and started racing again, and she broke into a cold sweat. She glanced toward the door, wondered if she could try to hobble out. She could see a pair of crutches abandoned on the other side of the room and she thought she could get those.

She tried to sit up straighter and managed it, but as soon as she tried to swing her legs out of bed a sharp, acute pain tore through her left thigh, starting in the foot she no longer had and travelling all the way up through her hip and the base of her spine.

Tyler had never been electrocuted before but she imagined the sensation would be quite similar.

Now she knew why the doctor had wanted to give her some morphine earlier. The anaesthetic in her system must have worn off obviously, and the simple act of trying to lift her leg had woken up all the raw nerves in it. Tyler gritted her teeth and tried not to cry out loud.

All of a sudden she was feeling dizzy and her vision had blurred. She gripped the railing on the side of the bed, leaning forward, willing herself not to be sick.

By the time the sergeant came back, she was drenched in sweat and breathing hard again. The doctor took one look at her and shook her head.

"It is a seven hour flight back to the UK," she said casually.

"Are you always this annoying, sergeant?" Tyler asked hotly. O'Connor flashed her a bright smile and reached into her pocket for a dose of morphine.

"It's always a good sign when patients start shouting at their doctor, I think."

She looked at Tyler, noticed sweat trickling down the middle of her forehead.

Her face had turned grey.

"Although you are not looking so good. Listen," she added, more gently this time. "I understand why you would want to remain awake and alert in a place like this, but I can assure you that you're safe."

Tyler threw her a look but she said nothing.

"Do you really want to spend seven hours on a plane feeling like this?"

"This won't last, will it?"

"I won't lie to you. It will get worse before it gets better. So I suggest you go for the full dose and enjoy the ride. What do you say, captain?"

It was the thought of not being able to stop worrying about Kate on the way out which made Tyler agree to the drug.

"Just don't give me too much," she muttered.

"Of course not," the doctor said brightly, and she injected her with the maximum dose.

Chapter Twelve

It took eight long weeks before Tyler started to grow stronger at last. She could hardly believe it had taken her so long. At first even spending as little as a couple of hours on crutches each day was more than she could handle. The sergeant at Bastion had lied, obviously.

She was not able to start her rehab as soon as she got to the UK, and for a while her recovery only seemed to be going backwards. It really floored her. In her mind she had expected to be in and out of rehab in record time. Reality was a different thing altogether, and she struggled to reconcile the two.

Initially she spent a lot of time in bed, mostly sleeping, fighting off a string of viruses and infections. She lost a lot of weight, got weaker.

After that her leg seemed to get worse, even though the doctors assured her that it was not the case. Sometimes the pain in her ankle and in her knee was so bad that Tyler had to touch her leg to remind herself that it was really gone. Every single nerve in her missing limb was screaming out, and on a couple of occasions she got such painful cramps that she blacked out.

Phantom pain they said. It was to be expected. It would get better.

They gave her morphine whenever she wanted it, and it helped a little, but not much. And she hated having to depend on it. Morphine also made her think of Kate, and that night in Cobel, and reminded her that despite her best intentions she had not been able to get in touch with her yet.

Still, at the start of her fourth week at Staunton things started to improve a little, and she got fitted with a high quality prosthetic leg. Frustratingly, the amount of time that she could spend practicing with it at first was extremely limited. Tyler felt enraged by the sluggishness of her own progress.

Her physiotherapist told her a million times that she had to be patient, that her leg had to heal properly first. It would come, but she could not rush the process.

There would be no shortcuts.

For the first time in her life Tyler found that her body would not do what she wanted it to do. Her head was racing ahead, but her body was stuck firmly behind.

Slowly but surely though she worked her way through recovery, and after five weeks she ditched her crutches and started using her prosthetic more.

She had adapted easily to Staunton's rehabilitation programme, a regime of eating, sleeping and relentless training. She was used to hard training sessions, except this time there were no runs on the beach, and instead it was all about core work and swimming. She swam twice a day, without fail, despite the advice of the physios who said that she was pushing herself too hard. But it was the only way that she could control the pain. She found that if she trained hard enough, and made herself feel tired enough, the pain in her lost leg was manageable without pain killers.

So they let it slide, and Tyler grew a little bit happier.

On a misty and gloomy December day, after finishing her second swim of the day, she made her way into the kitchen to see what was on offer. It was four o'clock in the afternoon and getting dark, and as pretty much always these days she found that she starving. With all the training she was doing the weight was literally falling off her, and chief cook Danielle had begun to bake vanilla cheesecakes on an industrial scale, just so that Tyler could have her daily treat.

Danielle was sixty-three, five two, always smiling, and as it happened, very willing to spent most of her spare time flirting with their new American resident.

"So D., when are you taking me out for dinner?" Tyler enquired as she walked in.

She was tired and she was using her crutches for once, and as Danielle turned to her she leaned them on the side of the counter, put both hands on it, and hoisted herself on top. She smiled, leaned her elbows on her thighs, and gave Danielle her full attention.

"I was waiting for you to take me out captain," Danielle shot back indignantly. "You eat so much my monthly wage would not cover the bill!"

She roared with laughter and moved closer to give Tyler a little poke on the shoulder.

"How come you're on crutches again, eh?" she asked.

"My leg hurts. I guess I just need to rest it a bit."

"How many miles you done in that swimming pool today?"

"Five today," Tyler replied.

Danielle shook her head in disapproval.

"No wonder your leg hurts. You nutter. Anyway, what brings you here then?"

"I just wanted to say hello, who do you take me for?" Tyler protested.

"A hungry swimmer. Sure you were not after some cake?"

"Me? Never!"

Tyler shook her head, clear grey eyes sparkling with mischief, enjoying the banter. Danielle raised her eyebrows at her and snorted.

"Fibber. You marines are the worst for that. Why don't you go sit in the dining room and I'll have a look in my cupboards and see what I can rustle up for you."

"Thanks D.," Tyler said gratefully, and she slid off the counter and grabbed her crutches. "I'm trying on a new running leg tomorrow morning," she added, almost shyly.

"About time! Then you can run on out of here and I can have a rest from feeding you!" Danielle exclaimed, faking relief.

She was happy when she got a genuine laugh out of Tyler, and she stepped forward to give her a quick hug.

"You have a lovely smile. You should use it more often," she said.

Dismissed, Tyler went to sit in the dining room, choosing a table at the back. She got on well with all the staff at Staunton, but she always preferred to be on her own when she was not training. She made sure to give Danielle an extra smile when the woman brought her a thick slice of cheesecake, and some strawberry compote to go with it.

"Cream?" Tyler asked hopefully.

"Don't push it girlie."

Tyler chuckled quietly. Danielle glanced back at her as she walked off, giving a little shake of the head. She felt for the young woman, who always seemed to be on her own. She had never once heard her complain, but there was a sadness in her eyes which was hard to ignore, and no amount of pretend banter had been able to fool Danielle so far.

"Excuse me, I'm looking for Captain Jackson?"

Danielle had been about to disappear back into the kitchen when she heard the voice behind her.

She turned and found herself facing a very beautiful woman, dressed in jeans and a pair of sturdy boots, and a black leather jacket. She had long, shiny black hair and bright, intelligent green eyes. She looked tired and excited all at the same time, and Danielle raised a suspicious eyebrow.

"Yes?" she said carefully.

The woman stared at her curiously for a second and then broke into a big smile.

"Sorry, I guess I really should introduce myself first, shouldn't I? I'm Lieutenant Ashley Peace," she said. "USMC."

"Another marine," Danielle muttered. "Guess you'll be wanting cheesecake too?"

The newcomer gave her a blank look and her eyes drifted slowly across the kitchen.

"Someone said Tyler might be around here somewhere?"

"That is correct."

The American woman cracked a little smile.

Security was tough in this place, she reflected, amused.

"Any chance you could point me in the right direction?" she asked.

Ashley walked straight into the large dining room, and she paused at the door as soon as she spotted Tyler. She took a slow breath, giving herself a couple of seconds to watch her friend.

Tyler sat alone at a table by the window, dressed in baggy jeans, a red hoodie that looked slightly too big for her, a pair of Nike on her feet. On her foot, Ashley corrected herself mentally. She bit her lip as she noticed how much weight Tyler had lost since she had last seen her, how it made her features look even sharper, more intense. Her hair had grown too and just brushed the base of her neck now. She was toying with a spoon and a piece of cake, staring into space, apparently lost in thought.

Smiling, Ashley took a few slow steps toward her.

"Hey, marine. If you're not hungry I'll gladly take it off your hands," she said quietly.

Tyler looked up, a hint of challenge in her eyes, looking annoyed at being disturbed. But as soon as her eyes fell on her visitor, her expression changed and she dropped her spoon in surprise.

"Ash?" she exclaimed.

The woman nodded and flashed her a happy grin.

A slow smile came to Tyler's lips, and she grabbed her crutches and stood up quickly. Her eyes on Ashley, she walked over to her friend, and as soon as she was close enough she let go of her clutches in one quick movement. She wrapped her arms around her and enfolded her in a tight hug.

"Ash," she murmured. "My God, are you really here?"

Ashley suddenly felt herself close to tears, unable to speak. So she simply nodded and returned the hug, crushing Tyler against her. It was a couple of seconds before she could say something.

"Oh, Ty, I am so sorry about what happened to you..." she murmured.

From the kitchen Danielle had heard the clatter of the crutches falling to the floor, and she rushed in, frowning in alarm. When she spotted the two women locked together in an embrace she relaxed, and watched them for a moment. Neither of them spoke, but Ashley's eyes were closed tightly, and Danielle noted how she had grabbed a handful of Tyler's hair and how hard she was holding on to her. Feeling more than a little bit curious, but reassured that everything was all right with the young captain, Danielle relaxed and walked away quietly.

Ashley had no idea how long they stood like that in silence, just holding on to each other. It felt like a long time, but also nowhere near long enough. Tyler's skin felt hot against hers, and she smelt of swimming pool and Deep Heat. All of a sudden Ashley struggled a little with the intensity of her emotions. The feel of Tyler's familiar body against hers stirred up memories Ashley knew were better left alone. After a while, she pulled away reluctantly. But she kept both hands on Tyler's arms, watching her, unable to stop grinning.

"Hey captain," she said softly.

"Hey marine. How are you?"

"Better now I've managed to find you," Ashley said frankly.

"I can't believe you're here," Tyler laughed, and she looked a little bit shell shocked at the same time. "How did you know…"

"I heard you'd been injured," Ashley interrupted. "Lenster's back home now. I bumped into him in San Anselmo and he told me all about it."

"Lenster," Tyler repeated with emotion, thinking of the young corporal she had left behind in Cobel. "Is he okay?"

"Yes. He's fine."

Tyler shook her head, her eyes growing a little bit distant as she thought about her men. They were home now. God. The weeks had flown by. She thought of Kate suddenly and wondered if that meant she was on her way back to the UK as well. As yet she had still not heard from her.

"Come," Ashley said softly. "Let's sit."

Tyler dropped back on to her chair and looked at her friend. She tried to remember how long it had been since she had last seen Ashley. A year, maybe two. Although they had been in touch on the phone and through email. Somehow it seemed as if Ashley had always been a part of her life. Through school and college, then the Marines. They had done their basic training together and completed their first tour of duty in Iraq in the same unit. Back home in San Francisco they were friends. Going out, going diving together. An image of Ashley naked in her bed at home flashed in front of Tyler's eyes.

She blinked and gave a light shake of the head.

"It's wonderful to see you Ash," she said with feeling.

"Likewise, buddy."

"So… what are you doing here?" Tyler enquired.

She frowned suddenly.

"Is everything okay?"

"Well, yes…"

"Sure?"

Ashley gave a light shrug.

"I got shot in the arm four months ago, and got sent home from

Helmand. But it's not the reason I'm here."

"Shit, I had no idea," Tyler exclaimed. "Why didn't you get in touch?"

"It's nothing," Ashley said calmly. "Plus, there was nothing you could have done about it, so I didn't want you to worry."

"Let me see," Tyler insisted.

Her expression tightened as Ashley slipped her arm out of her sleeve and showed her the long scar on the inside of her bicep, that snaked its way all the way down her forearm.

"It looks bad, Ash," Tyler muttered. "How are you doing?"

"I'm fine. Radial nerve is sort of busted though."

Tyler raised a worried eyebrow.

"What does that mean for your career?" she asked.

"Well, my days in the military are over."

"What..."

"Don't worry, please," Ashley interrupted, leaning forward to rest her hand on Tyler's forearm. "I'm fine. I wanted to get out anyway."

"You did?" Tyler was amazed. "You never said."

"Well, it has been a while since I last saw you, Ty."

She looked up when Danielle appeared at her side, with another portion of cake and two steaming mugs of coffee.

"Oh, thank you."

"You are very welcome darling."

"Thanks D.," Tyler said, smiling.

"Don't get used to the special treatment," Danielle shot back, "and if you girls are going to start taking your clothes off, kindly take it to your room please, captain."

Tyler's face coloured a dark shade of pink, and Ashley cast an amused glance in her direction.

"Sorry. Not been here five minutes and I'm already getting you into trouble," she observed.

"As usual. Although not hard to do, Danielle is an expert," Tyler acknowledged. "I think she'd make a terrifying drill instructor."

"Looks like she really likes you."

Tyler gave a light shrug.

"I'm glad you seem to be okay with all this," she said, but the emotion in her voice was obvious.

Ashley nodded. Breaking the moment, she grabbed her spoon and handed it to her.

"Eat," she ordered with a smile. "You look like you need to."

"Feels like all I do is eat these days," Tyler stated moodily.

She started to dig into her cake anyway. Ashley glanced at her, her eyes softening as she noted the impatient look that flashed across her eyes as she spoke. Patience had never been Tyler's strong suit.

"I take it the training load here is pretty heavy?" she asked.

"It's okay. Lots of swimming, core work, physio work... Sort of like a full time job."

"Nothing you can't handle I presume?"

"It's not as hard as running the fire tracks back at home with twenty pounds of kit on my back. Not as much fun either."

Tyler smiled a little, and Ashley wondered if she was aware of how sad she looked. Her eyes drifted to her leg and she felt her heart tighten. She wanted to have a look at it, but she refrained from touching her.

"So how are you feeling?" she asked instead.

Tyler gave a light shrug. She dropped her spoon and leaned back in her chair. Her automatic response these days was always to say that she was fine. Because she was, and she would be. She saw people every day in the gym who had come back a lot worse off than she was. Double, triple amputees, guys who were blind, completely paralysed, burnt. She was one of the lucky ones, and she was intensely aware of it.

"At the end of the day, it's just a foot," she concluded. "It'll be fine."

"Yes, you're right," Ashley agreed. "It could have been a lot worse. But I want to hear about you, not about everybody else."

She smiled at Tyler and held her gaze, searching deep into her eyes.

"So how are you?" she asked again.

Tyler exhaled slowly. She had forgotten that when Ashley asked a question, she did not let people off until she was satisfied that she had got the full, honest answer. And she was not afraid to ask the hard questions either. A bit like Kate, really.

Tyler tried to smile, and surprised herself when she failed. There was a lump in her throat, and she coughed and took a sip of coffee.

"Sorry. Uh... Yeah, I'm fine," she stammered.

Ashley moved her chair closer to hers. She lay her palm on top of her good leg.

"Really," she said softly. "It's me you're talking to. So come on, captain. Spill."

Tyler hesitated, feeling her resolve to keep it all in and put a brave face on crumble.

"Okay. Well... For starters, my career is over," she said.

Her voice was hard, and Ashley could hear the hurt in it, anger and resentment simmering, boiling really, just below the surface.

"I thought I could go back, you know?" Tyler said. "I thought once I'd done all the rehab, and if I managed to get back to full fitness, that I would be able to keep my job."

Ashley nodded, knowing what would come next. Not many people who lost a limb ever went back on operations again or even remained into active service.

Tyler of all people would have known that. But Ashley also knew how hard she would have fought to become an exception to the rule.

"I can get out, honorable discharge etc., or I can spend the rest of my career behind a desk filling out paperwork and stuff."

"I'm sorry, Ty. What are you going to do?

"It's a no brainer. I hate paperwork."

Ashley was not surprised. She rubbed Tyler's leg in sympathy, green eyes shining with kindness.

"The Marines will finance any retraining I want to do, so at least that is something to fall back on."

"Absolutely. That is great news."

Ashley's tone was warm and encouraging. Tyler nodded without enthusiasm.

"Yeah, that's great," she muttered.

Her eyes focused on a spot on the wall behind her friend.

"I'll be okay," she said with a shrug. "I'm not worried about making ends meet. But Collins…"

"What about him?" Ashley asked softly.

Tyler pursed her lips and refused to meet her eyes.

"I won't forgive them for Ben. No way."

"Forgive who?"

"The Taliban. If I could, I'd get on the first plane back, grab a machine gun and just blast them all out of existence…"

"Hey," Ashley interrupted, alarmed. "Come on. That's not the way, you know that."

She leaned forward and rested her finger under Tyler's chin, turning her head gently until she could look into her eyes.

"Tell me you don't mean that," she said softly.

Tyler exhaled sharply.

"I don't know, Ash," she said. "I just…"

She rubbed her eyes, and shook her head a little. Sometimes when she thought about the friends she had lost to Afghanistan, the anger she felt was so strong it just overwhelmed her. But as she looked at Ashley now and noticed the concerned look in her eyes, mixed with compassion, and gentleness, images flashed in her mind of some of the villagers she had met. Some of the kids she had played with. All the smiles, all the encounters, all the real people who were caught in a horrible war they did not want. These were the ones she would always remember.

Tyler had never been really good at holding on to her anger, and almost as if by magic it disappeared.

"No, I guess I don't mean it," she admitted finally.

Sighing, she leaned forward and rested her elbows on her thighs.

"It just feels like a dream, Ash," she mumbled. "You know?"

"Yeah. I know."

Tyler looked at her friend, her eyes intent and hoping for some answers.

"I can't remember much about what happened on that day, it's driving me nuts. Did Lenster say anything to you?"

Ashley took a deep breath, thinking back to when the man had related the events of a day he called the worst one of his life so far.
She leaned a little closer to Tyler, rested her hand on her shoulder and spoke in a quiet voice.

"He said the suicide bomber grabbed Ben just before he detonated. That Ben wrestled with him for a second and tried to drag him away from you..."

Tyler winced at those words and she shivered. She had wondered about that, wondered about why she had come off so lightly when Collins had lost his life. She was not surprised to hear that at the very last second, her friend had tried to protect her. She wished he had run away instead and saved himself.

Ashley decided to leave out the part when Lenster had told her about the smell. Of burnt flesh and blood, and body parts scattered all across the field.

"What else did Lenster say?" Tyler insisted.

Ashley sighed a little.

"He saw Ben..."

She hesitated, not sure how much to reveal.

In the end she decided to go with the short version.

"He wouldn't have known a thing, Ty."

Tyler shook her head.

"I don't know if that's not worse, in a way," she observed

darkly. "To not even be aware. I think I would want to know it's coming."

Ashley tightened her grip on her shoulder and gently brushed a tear from her cheek.

"Hey, come on," she said softly. "It won't help to dwell on these things. It won't help you to get bitter about it."

She watched as Tyler shook her head, looking lost in thoughts again.

"Have you spoken to any of the other guys yet?" she asked.

"No. Although I tried to call Ben's wife several times," Tyler said slowly.

"How is she doing?"

"She's refusing to talk to me."

Ashley looked confused.

"Why would she not want to talk to you?" she asked.

Tyler hesitated.

"She thinks it's my fault that Ben was killed," she said eventually.

"That's ridiculous!" Ashley exclaimed, instantly angry on her friend's behalf. "Why on earth would she think that?"

"She needs someone to blame I guess. And she's right. I should have been more careful."

Tyler had grown incredibly pale, and uncertainty shone in her eyes.

"What? Tyler, come on," Ashley exclaimed in disbelief. "There was no way you could have known."

Tyler shook her head, looking far from convinced, and Ashley felt it when she started to tremble.

"Come on," she murmured. "Don't get upset."

"I knew there was something off with that guy Ash," Tyler said quietly. "I just didn't figure it out quickly enough. So yeah, I made a mistake. I was in charge, and I let Ben down."

Ashley stared at her for a moment, considering the madness of that comment. Tyler was convinced that her friend's death at the hands of a suicide bomber was her fault. This was a clear sign that she was not doing as well as Ashley had hoped she would be, not as well as Tyler would have wanted everyone to think, and it was time to do something about it.

Ashley pushed her chair back and stood up.

"Okay. I don't know about you, but I think that's enough of the heavy stuff for now," she declared.

Tyler looked up at her, making no effort to move.

"So what do you want to do about it?" she asked, and she sounded a little annoyed.

"Hey, don't get mad at me, okay?" Ashley told her softly.

"Sorry. And you still haven't told me what you're doing here."

Ashley stepped forward, and she pulled Tyler up with her as well. She wrapped her arms tightly around her waist again and exhaled slowly.

"I wanted to see you. When I heard about what happened... Shit, Tyler, did you really think I was going to stay away?"

Tyler finally relaxed into the embrace.

"No," she said, smiling a little.

Being with Ashley felt just like coming home. It was amazing, and yet something was missing.

Tyler thought of Kate and her heart tightened.

"Have you got a prosthetic yet?" Ashley asked, her breath warm against the side of her neck.

"Yes."

"How are you getting on with it?"

"Kind of shuffling along."

Ashley pulled back and flashed her a bright smile.

"Cool. How about you put it on and I take you out to dinner. I've got a business proposition for you."

NATALIE DEBRABANDERE

PART TWO

Chapter Thirteen

Sausset Beach, South of France.
Eight months later.

"Are you sure you know how to do this?" Kate asked, trying hard not to burst out laughing.

She watched as her friend Marion fiddled with the rear view mirror of their French hire car, switched on the wipers, swore, turned them off, did it again.

"What, drive on the wrong side of the road?" Marion shot back with a confident wink. "Please. Have some faith."

"Just making sure, cos it's looking a bit iffy right now mate. Just saying."

"I learnt how to drive a tank when I was based at Catterick. So don't you worry, I can handle this wee little thing."

Kate opened the window and rested her arm on the frame, laughing at her friend's determined attitude. She was not army for nothing, she thought, amused. Marion looked back at her, pleased to see her looking relaxed for once.

Kate had returned from Afghanistan in one piece, but she was changed. Thoughtful. A little distant and withdrawn. Most of all, sad.

"Are you enjoying yourself mate?" she asked.

"I am. Thanks for bullying me into this, I do appreciate it."

"Ha! You're welcome. You are going to love Provence. And then in between scuba diving sessions and exploring the back country, perhaps you can find yourself a girlfriend for the holiday."

"I already have a girlfriend for the holiday," Kate said.

Marion threw her a stern look.

"You know what I mean. One you can have wild, passionate, crazy sex with."

"As if," Kate snorted.

"Why not, mate?"

"That's not what I'm looking for."

"Again, why not?"

"I'm happy on my own."

"Kate. I don't believe that for a second. You don't look happy for a start."

Kate simply shrugged.

"I'm fine."

Marion started in on the now familiar, gentle lecture.

"You need to move on, Katie, it's been almost a year now. Dwelling on that woman from Afghan isn't going to get you anywhere. You know that, right?"

Kate frowned at the mention of Tyler.

"I mean, if she had been even slightly interested in seeing you again she would have left contact details, right?"

Kate sighed a little and pursed her lips. She remembered how devastated she had been when she had finally made it to Staunton, only to be told that Tyler had already left. That she had been with a beautiful American woman when she had checked out of the rehab centre. And that she had not said where she was going or how she could be contacted.

She had simply vanished.

"Am I right?" Marion insisted.

"I guess so," Kate said, feeling deflated. "I mean, I am not holding out for her, you know…"

She felt a tightening in her chest as she said that and shook her head. *I just miss her so much*, she thought. *I just wish I could make sure that she is okay.*

Disappearing like this…

It was so unlike Tyler.

"Well, that's good then," Marion declared.

She took her eyes off the road long enough to flash Kate a warm smile, and she reached for her hand and gave her a heartfelt squeeze.

"I just want you to have a good time, okay? Try to relax when we are there, and let's just see what happens. Yes?"

Kate nodded, ran a hand through her hair, and smiled.

"Yes," she said with conviction. "Absolutely."

When Marion had mentioned a "dive boat", Kate had not imagined that they would get one as luxurious as the 120 foot catamaran she was now looking at. She loved boats, and that particular one looked amazing. It was a double decker with a full beam cabin at the front and an enlarged fly bridge. The mast was mounted on top. It looked sleek, comfortable and spacious, and Kate shook her head a little.

She was in awe.

"Wow," she commented thoughtfully. "Not just any old RIB, eh?"

"Nope. Only the best for us, darling. You like?"

"I love it," Kate said with a huge grin.

"Come on then, let's get on board."

The two women were part of a group of six learner divers aiming to get PADI qualified. The woman in charge of the dive school was fifty two year old Cathy DeMatteo, a local French woman.

She had three other instructors on board with them, which ensured that each trainer would be in charge of no more than one pair of students.

DeMatteo was a tall, no nonsense sort of woman with a cracking sense of humour, and a gift for making everybody feel comfortable. She had short cropped black hair, blue eyes, she smiled a lot, and she spoke perfect English punctuated by incomprehensible French exclamations and lots of hand movement.

Kate relaxed as soon as they were on their way out of the harbour. When the dive brief started, she felt the tension of the past few months start to ease up a little. She smiled at Marion, and chuckled at the happy twinkle she saw in her eyes.

"Thanks mate, this is great," she whispered in her ear.

DeMatteo explained that for the first day they would anchor off not far from Sausset, in a sheltered cove, and everybody would get familiarised with the diving equipment. Nice and easy. The boat was magnificent, the weather fantastic. Kate felt quietly excited when she thought of the few weeks in Provence ahead of her now.

That is, until the instructors were introduced.

The first two were a tall French guy and a fit looking American woman. Kate did not really hear their names or qualifications as DeMatteo introduced them to the group and assigned them to their pairs. Her eyes were on the woman who got introduced next as chief diver.

As the ex-marines captain came to the front and gave a quick smile and a friendly wave to the group, Kate looked away sharply. A rush of emotions assaulted her. Relief was one of them. Panic was not too far off. She briefly wondered why. After all she had done nothing wrong.

When she looked back, after what seemed like ages, Tyler was standing right in front of her and Marion. Her bright, intense grey eyes were fixed firmly on Kate. She looked as surprised as Kate felt and also a little bit uncomfortable.

"Kate, Marion, you'll be with Ty," DeMatteo declared.

Kate remained rooted to the spot, unable to move. Next to her, Marion was introducing herself, grabbing Tyler's hand, obviously pleased with the pairing for reasons that had nothing to do with diving, Kate knew. Tyler chatted politely to her, stealing glances at Kate a couple of times.

"So, this is my friend, Kate," Marion said, keen to introduce her.

But her smile faded as soon as she saw the devastated look on her face.

"Hey, what's wrong?" she exclaimed, alarmed.

Kate gave her a quick, reassuring smile.

"Nothing, don't worry," she said.

She blinked hard, fighting to keep her composure, and she turned to face Tyler.

"Hello."

Her voice was hard when she spoke. She was surprised by that, because it was sadness she felt. But she noticed in the way that Tyler hesitated that she had obviously come across as angry.

"Hi Kate," the ex-officer said in a low voice.

Then she hesitated again.

Marion was looking from one woman to the other, a mixture of concern and curiosity in her eyes.

"Ty, you got a minute?" DeMatteo shouted from across the deck.

"Yeah," Tyler yelled back. "I'll be right back," she said, mainly to Kate, holding her gaze just long enough to get herself a curt nod in reply.

Marion grabbed her friend's arm as soon as she left, and turned to her urgently.

"What's wrong?" she asked. "I thought you were okay, and now all of a sudden you look like you've seen a ghost."

"Something like that."

"Do you two know each other?"

"It's her, mate," Kate said slowly, her eyes on Tyler as she stood talking quietly to her boss on the other side of the boat.

"Her who?" Marion repeated, looking puzzled.

"It's Tyler."

"You mean the marine from Cobel? *That* Tyler?"

Kate gave a silent nod.

Marion frowned and stopped talking, turning back to gaze at Tyler. The woman was wearing jeans, a black tank top, and trainers on her feet. She looked fit and strong, sexy, and certainly not disabled in any way.

"I thought you told me she had lost a leg," Marion said.

Kate exhaled sharply.

"She did. She has a limp. You can see it if you look hard enough, although she is very good with that prosthetic she's wearing now."

She stared at Tyler, emotion making her heart grow tight. *God, she looks stunning*, she thought. She had lost some weight but not a lot of muscle. Her hair had grown lighter in the Provence sunshine. She looked tanned and healthy, and just every bit as handsome as she had when they were in Afghanistan. It was hard for Kate not to react to her physically.

She had a sudden flashback of the last time she had seen Tyler, barely conscious, covered in dirt, and bleeding to death in a cold Afghan field. She felt her knees weaken at the memories, and emotions threatened to overwhelm her once more.

"I'm sorry mate," Marion murmured, sounding as if this was somehow her fault, and not really sure how to handle the situation. "I guess this is not really how you expected to bump into her again, right?"

"No. Not at all," Kate snapped.

Her friend just stared at her in silence.

"What are you going to do now?" she asked after a few seconds.

Kate looked at her and took a deep breath. She knew how much Marion had been looking forward to this trip, how much she wanted to learn to dive, and how much she had been looking forward to going away with her. Tyler had made her choice. It had nothing to do with her, and certainly nothing to do with Marion.

"Don't worry," she said. "I am going to get this sorted, and you and I are going to have a fantastic holiday."

"We could cancel, Kate…"

"Absolutely not."

Kate spotted Tyler carrying a couple of dive cylinders inside the boat, and she seized her opportunity.

"Give me five minutes, all right? I'm going to get this squared away."

"Are you going to kiss her or punch her?" Marion said softly.

"Neither," Kate muttered.

She found Tyler below deck in the equipment room, leaning against the wall staring into space. She had obviously sought refuge in there to get over the shock of their earlier encounter, and she jumped when she spotted Kate.

She stood silently, not sure what she was supposed to say and more or less waiting for Kate to initiate the conversation. She looked a little bit nervous, and her skin was glowing from the effort of carrying the cylinders. Kate found just the sight of her took her breath away, and this was not how she wanted to be feeling, right this very minute.

"Hello Tyler," she said lightly.

"Hey doc," Tyler replied in the same tone.

She bit her lip, realising that the friendly nickname might not be welcome now. She could not resist looking at Kate, and Kate felt her pulse quicken when she noticed Tyler's gaze travel slowly over her body. The familiar grey eyes were like a caress over her naked shoulders, and lingered over her breasts for an instant. Kate swallowed hard. Then Tyler blinked a couple of times and her gaze fell on the thick red scar still visible on Kate's arm.

She frowned and took an impulsive step forward.

"How is your arm?" she asked intently.

Kate glanced at it, as if remembering it for the first time. She shrugged. *As if you care,* she wanted to say. But she suspected that Tyler did. That was the problem. She knew the woman cared. And yet she had abandoned her without a single word of explanation.

Kate was hurting.

"Arm's all mended," she acknowledged. Then, in spite of herself, she added: "You did a good job with the stitches."

Tyler nodded and her eyes cleared a little.

"Good, I'm glad to hear it."

"How is your leg?"

"It's uh… fine. It's fine," Tyler stammered.

Her expression was one of total powerlessness.

Right now Kate was her only link to Cobel. She had buried every other one. She had wanted to forget everything about it so badly, and yet seeing the medic brought it all back, and all she wanted to do right now was remember.

Talk about it, go over it, try to make sense of it.

She took a hard breath and stepped forward a little more. Her eyes sparkled. To hell with being reserved and polite as if we do not know each other, those eyes seemed to say. To hell with barriers.

Kate watched her coming a little closer, as if in a trance, thinking she should move, or at least say something.

"Tyler…" she whispered.

Brought back to reality by some noise outside the door, Tyler stopped only inches from Kate, breathing hard.

"Hey buddy, you in there? Cathy wants to know if you're ready to go…"

Kate turned her head, immensely annoyed at being disturbed.

The other woman instructor, whose name she could not remember and did not care to know appeared at the door, and stopped dead in her tracks when she saw Kate and Tyler standing so close to each other.

Ashley raised an eyebrow, not really sure from their expression what the two women had been doing. Neither of them looked happy.

"Hmm... You okay ladies?" she asked.

But her eyes were on Tyler only.

Concerned, searching.

"Yes, I'll be right with you Ash," Tyler said quickly, sounding tense.

Ashley narrowed her eyes at her, and threw a questioning, slightly suspicious look toward Kate.

"Right. Okay then," she said somehow unhappily, and left.

Kate felt herself grow angry and she could not help herself.

"Is that your girlfriend?" she said sharply.

"No. Of course not. This is my friend Ash. She's..."

"Yeah, right. Whatever," Kate interrupted. "It's none of my business anyway."

Tyler's eyes clouded over.

Their moment was gone.

"That's right, it isn't," she said in a low voice, and the rebuke brought fresh tears to Kate's eyes.

She brushed them off angrily.

"So here's the thing," she snapped. "My friend Marion, she's the one who used to send me shampoo and stuff at Cobel. You remember?"

Tyler was hurt that Kate even thought she had to ask. As if she could forget anything about Cobel. It haunted her, night and day, and there was nothing she could do about it. The sleepless nights, the constant nightmares, the panic attacks which had become more frequent after she had lost her leg.

She started to get angry.

"Yeah, I remember," she said darkly.

Kate stared hard at her.

"Well. Marion's been looking forward to this trip with me for a long time now, and there is absolutely no way I am going to cancel it."

"No reason why you should, Kate. Listen, you look upset, can we just..."

"I'm not upset, Tyler," Kate exclaimed.

She exhaled sharply, shook her head and was silent. She was handling this extremely badly, she knew it, but right this second she did not want to be in the same room with Tyler. She had thought she would want to, but this was just too hard.

Tyler took a long look at her, and her expression grew sad. Talking to Kate right now felt like talking to a brick wall. Whatever connection they had once had, it appeared to have been severed for good.

She took a deliberate step back, and dropped the shutters down on her heart. She was good at that. She switched off her emotions, disconnected her feelings, and almost separated from her own self. She did it just the way she used to do when she was a marine shooting at the enemy, when she was killing people she could not afford to care about. When she spoke again she was as cold as ice and feeling absolutely nothing.

"I can get you reassigned to another instructor," she said quietly.

"That would be great."

Tyler simply shrugged.

"Okay, I'll do that."

"Thank you."

And then Kate walked away quickly, leaving her alone in the middle of the room.

Chapter Fourteen

True to her word, all of Kate's energies over the following days were focused on making sure that Marion had a good time. Tyler had obviously put in a quiet request with DeMatteo, and the pair were reassigned to a different instructor, without any fuss being made.

Unusually, Tyler was absent from most of the theory sessions, and it was obvious that she was doing her best to stay in the background and give Kate and her friend the space that Kate has requested. She hated doing it, keeping that distance between them, but she did it anyway because she realised that it was what Kate wanted. She tried to convince herself that it was better that way anyway.

"I've only got myself to blame for this," she admitted to Ashley one evening.

They were on her boat, her new home where she had no reminders of her previous life in the Marines, and the people she had known back then.

Ashley remembered when her friend had bought it, it had been just an ugly empty shell, the decks bare and the walls just dull grey metal. During her first few weeks in France Tyler had worked on it relentlessly, almost day and night, to transform it into a magnificent home. The work had been good for her body, and good for her soul. Now the catamaran boasted new wooden decks throughout, and one entire side of the cabin was made of glass, overlooking the open sea and Marseille and the Chateau d'If in the distance.

It was very private as well, which appealed to Tyler. She had managed to bag herself the only mooring in the entire harbour where she was not overlooked, and no one was able to snoop. The boat also had a reasonably sized galley kitchen, and a large bedroom with ensuite farther down below. Green plants were everywhere, and other than that the decor was clean and minimalist. Ashley absolutely loved it, and often after a diving session she would come on board and cook with Tyler.

"What do you mean you've only got yourself to blame?" she asked, looking at her now as she slammed a bunch of vegetables on the counter.

"I left Staunton in a big rush, and I made damn sure she couldn't find me."

Ashley gave a small shrug.

"Yeah, you did a runner. Then again, probably what you needed to do at the time, right, buddy?"

She remembered how unstable Tyler had been during her final days at Staunton, and even during the first few weeks in France. She had settled a little now, but Ashley knew it would not take much to drag her down the path of depression.

Tyler simply shrugged, her back to her friend, staring unseeingly out of the window at the glittering blue sea in front of her. Ashley spotted the tension in her shoulders. Tyler was holding onto the knife so tightly her knuckles had turned white.

Ashley gave a soft sigh and tried again.

"Kate is here now Ty," she reminded her gently.

"It doesn't matter."

"Of course it does."

"No. I fucked up, end of story."

"Okay, I get that's what you believe. But this is a second chance for you, isn't it? Take it."

Tyler shook her head.

"No. It's too late," she repeated, looking pale as she did.

Ashley observed her as she moved around the kitchen. She was well aware of her friend's history, and she felt immense sympathy for her. At the same time, she knew that sympathy would not do much for Tyler right now.

"Hey captain."

"Don't call me that."

"Why not?"

Tyler went still, and finally met Ashley's eyes.

"You know why," she said tightly.

"Why? Cos you quit the Marines?"

Tyler slammed her knife down on the counter, so hard it sent pain shooting up her arm and into her shoulder.

"I didn't quit," she exclaimed.

Her voice was unsteady.

Ashley eyed her calmly, and gave a slow shake of the head.

"You didn't quit; but you didn't fight for it either."

"What do you mean? What the fuck am I supposed to do with only one leg? Join the Navy Seals!?"

Tyler was livid. She looked around the room for something else to slam and found nothing. For a second she looked as if she would go for Ashley. But then she grew still and she pursed her lips as tears burned the back of her eyes.

"Ash, I didn't quit," she repeated.

It made Ashley feel sad to see the beaten look in Tyler's eyes.

"I'm sorry."

She walked up to her quickly and wrapped her arms around her. But Tyler felt as unyielding as a block of granite, and she did not return the hug.

"I know you didn't. But coming to bury yourself down here with me is just as good as," Ashley said carefully.

She pulled back a little until she could look her in the eye. Tyler looked angry now. Anybody with any sense would have backed down from the argument. But it would take more than this to make Ashley go quiet.

"Oh come on," she argued. "There you are, being given a second chance with the woman you love, and what do you do? Hide."

"I am not in love with her."

"Of course you are," Ashley exclaimed, her eyes wide.

"No. I am not. And I don't need anyone," Tyler said angrily, eyes flashing. "And that..."

She stopped herself before she could say the unthinkable. She had nearly blurted out *that goes for you, too.* Sensing where this was all going, Ashley headed for the door, looking back only once.

"Stop running, Tyler," she said flatly. "Can't you see it's not too late? Do something about it before she leaves, or you will regret it for the rest of your life."

Tyler did not sleep well, nightmares and pain in her leg keeping her awake most of the night. She finally gave up trying as it neared four o'clock and got up. She felt like punching something. Three times now she had had to replace the door to her bedroom cupboard because she had punched a hole through it. Before she could give in to that again, she quickly put on a pair of shorts and a T-shirt, grabbed her running leg, and hit the road.

She needed some time alone to think.

As she ran through the still dark and empty streets of the village, headed for the hills, she mentally went through the past few months in her head.

When Ashley had come to find her at Staunton she had explained that she was starting a diving school in France with DeMatteo. She had offered Tyler a part in the business, and Tyler had accepted immediately.

She had done it because it represented a fresh start for her, and the opportunity to leave the Marines behind for good.

At least that was the official story.

She was desperate for a simple life in France. Diving for a living, taking people out sea kayaking, running in the hills above Sausset.

She owned a third of the school and she loved living on the boat. She did not want a relationship. She did not want to get involved.

The truth was that she had known if she gave Kate a way to get in touch with her, that Kate would want more. And Tyler did not know how to do this. She was convinced that if she allowed herself to fall for Kate even more than she already had, and something happened, that she would not be able to pull it back together this time. So disappearing over to France with Ashley had been her escape route, as well as the easy way out. She had run.

And now it looked as if it had all been for nothing, because not only was Kate back in her life, sort of, but now she had lost her friendship as well.

Tyler gritted her teeth as she thought about this particular fact, feeling her stomach churn as she attacked the final part of the hill.

She did not stop as she got to the top, and started on the descent immediately, breathing deep and concentrating on not losing her balance. It was harder running off road with her specially designed leg, but she had done this run many times before, and she was back down in the village in under twenty minutes.

As she ran steadily toward the beach, she glanced in the direction of the hotel where Kate and Marion were staying. She remembered their time at Cobel and how beautiful Kate always looked first thing in the morning.

How funny she was. How tender, and caring.

Conditions at Cobel had been rough, and Tyler remembered it as one of the worst periods of her military career, for obvious reasons. But somehow, thanks of Kate, she also had some of the best memories of her entire life.

She slowed down as she reached the beach, drenched in sweat, her leg throbbing, but feeling a lot calmer than before. Her run had restored some kind of hope.

Tyler was glad to see that it was still too early for most people and that she had the place to herself. There was a swimmer out though, quite far, and this was unusual. Tyler watched her for a moment, pretty sure that it was Marion.

She had heard Kate mention her friend's early morning swims, and Tyler had almost cut in to say that swimming alone was not the best idea in the world, especially with the hidden currents around the harbour. But she knew that her comments were likely to be ignored, so she had kept quiet.

Now as she watched Marion's uneven and laboured stroke she wished she had spoken out when she had the chance. She noticed how the woman seemed to be slowing down as she neared the harbour. She looked anything but comfortable out there. Tyler saw her look toward the beach a couple of times, then start swimming again. She seemed to be struggling more and more.

Tyler glanced around and confirmed that they were indeed the only two people out.

"Shit," she muttered under her breath.

She grabbed her mobile and dialled Ashley's number. Just as her friend came on the line, Tyler clearly saw Marion go under.

"I'm at the beach. Marion's in trouble, come quick," she said immediately.

She did not wait for an answer. She dropped her phone, ran into the water, and when she was far enough away she got rid of her prosthetic and threw it back, not looking where it landed.

She was an excellent swimmer, and the leg would only slow her down. She trusted herself to get to Marion in time to help. She went for it and she went hard. When she reached the point where she had seen her go under, she dipped her head under water, searching for her. Seeing nothing, she turned around and just caught sight of her surfacing a little way away.

She had drifted. She was drifting away from the beach quite rapidly now.

"Marion!" Tyler shouted. "Hang on!"

But the woman gave no sign that she had heard or even seen her.

Gasping, she disappeared under again. This time Tyler had her eyes on her, and she kicked vigorously and dived after her.

Marion appeared to be unconscious and she was sinking fast. Tyler only just managed to catch up with her. She immediately wrapped one arm around her waist, and they were still sinking. Using her free arm and leg, Tyler started to swim them back toward the surface. It was slow going and a fair way up, and she had expended a huge amount of energy on the way down. Marion was heavy and totally unresponsive. Tyler suddenly realised there was a real possibility that she might not be able to make it. She was running out of oxygen. Refusing to give up, she kicked harder, feeling her lungs burning. By the time she broke through the surface she could see black spots dancing in front of her eyes.

But they had made it.

Gasping for air, Tyler looked around and spotted people on the beach. She knew Ashley would be one of them. Help was on the way. Dismayed to realise that they had drifted even farther away from the beach, she started to swim them back, fighting against the current that was doing its best to drag them out to sea. It would have been very tempting to just stop and drift, but she needed to get Marion back to shore fast.

"Hey, can you hear me?" she panted.

There was no reply.

"Marion. Come on. Wake up!"

It took a few seconds, and then Marion started to come round. As soon as she felt her move against her Tyler glanced quickly back. The woman's eyes were still closed but she was showing signs of waking up. Tyler breathed easier all of a sudden. Her energy was coming back.

"That's it," she said, encouragingly against the woman's ear. "Keep breathing, that's right."

Marion's eyes fluttered open. Still believing that she was drowning, she gasped and struggled against Tyler.

"Don't..." Tyler started, only to go silent when Marion inadvertently hit her in the mouth with her elbow.

Surprised, Tyler lost her grip on her and swallowed a mouthful of water. Then Marion threw her arms around her neck, pushing her down below the surface. For God's sake! Tyler thought. If Marion carried on like this she would be the one drowning. She managed to free herself and as soon as she resurfaced she reached for her again. The woman was breathing hard, not completely aware of what she was doing. Tyler struggled to catch her breath, but she did not fight her.

"Just relax, I've got you," she repeated, as calmly as she could. "Help is on the way. I've got you, okay, Marion?"

It took a few more seconds before Marion started to calm down. Things came back into focus. She stared at Tyler, and suddenly realised was she was doing.

It was obvious that the diving instructor was out of breath and struggling to keep them both on the surface.

"Sorry," she exclaimed, sounding panicked. "I'm sorry."

She swallowed some more water and Tyler again asked her to calm down.

"Just hold on to me," she repeated. "It's okay. Take your time."

Marion released her grip a little and Tyler relaxed.

"You're all right?" she asked.

She kept a close eye on the woman, whose face was as white as a sheet.

"You were unconscious, what happened out there?"

Marion took a hard breath. One minute she was swimming on her own, the next she was holding on to Tyler for dear life. What happened in between was a bit of a blur.

"I got cramp... I think," she said. "Swallowed some water. I'm not sure..."

Ashley caught up with them then.

"All right Tyler?" she asked immediately.

Her voice was calm and controlled, but her gaze was sharp as she focused on her friend, her concern for her obvious.

"I'm hanging out," Tyler admitted, and Ashley quickly replaced her at Marion's side.

"Can you make it back okay on your own if I stay with her?" she asked.

"Yeah, okay."

"Are you sure?"

Tyler nodded, and Ashley helped an exhausted Marion swim the little distance back to the beach. Someone had called an ambulance and the paramedics took over from her immediately. Ashley ran to retrieve Tyler's prosthetic, shook the sand out of it, and helped her shuffle out of the water slowly.

"Thanks Ash."

"No problem. Sure you're all right?"

"Yes, no worries."

Tyler sat down and adjusted her prosthetic. Then she leaned back and angled her face toward the sun, feeling exhausted all of a sudden.

Ashley squatted down by her side.

"Hey, you gotta work on that fitness of yours," she teased.

Tyler failed to see the joke in that.

"Only kidding, Ty. That was an awesome rescue."

"How is she?"

"She's all right. Scared herself I think, but other than that she's okay."

"Scared me," Tyler murmured. "She could have drowned, Ash." Tyler looked back toward the ambulance, her eyes filling with tears at the thought. Being ignored by Kate and having to stay away and pretend that she was not desperate to talk to her was taking its toll.

Her emotions were all over the place.

"She didn't drown," Ashley pointed out gently. "Thanks to you."

Tyler rubbed her eyes, feeling the familiar dark thoughts looming over her, taking hold.

"I almost didn't make it," she said. "Talk about some useless cripple!"

"Hey, knock it off."

Ashley's expression was serious as she knelt in front of her friend. She stared hard at her.

"Useless cripple, my ass. You saved her life. Don't beat yourself up about what could have been, okay?"

She could tell by the look in Tyler's eyes that she was not getting through to her.

She tried to think of ways to help.

"By the way, Kate was asking after you," she said eventually.

Tyler's hands shook a little at the mention of Kate.

"Really? Tell her I'm fine."

Ashley's expression did not change, but she shook her head a little.

"You tell her," she murmured.

She turned and smiled at Kate, who was standing behind them, a safe distance away, giving them plenty of space.

"Hi. She's all yours," she said.

Tyler stood up quickly, nearly losing her balance in the process. Ashley grabbed her and steadied her, shot her a warning look, her trademark "don't you dare fuck this up" look, and then walked away leaving the two of them alone.

"Hey, Tyler."

"Hi. How is your friend?" Tyler asked with a quick glance toward the ambulance.

"She's fine," Kate said with relief. "She said she got cramp in her leg and swallowed some water, and before she knew it she was going down. Skipped breakfast as well which didn't help."

"Yeah. That's how fast it can happen. Tell her not to go swimming alone again, please. It's not safe here."

It was the longest conversation Kate had had with Tyler since that first day on the boat, when she had pretty much just ranted at her. Her thoughts drifted back to that morning in Afghanistan when they had first met. She remembered the evening she got shot, and Tyler's forlorn expression that night just before she had fallen asleep in her arms. She had that same look in her eyes now, and Kate felt her heart tighten. It was so hard to keep her distance. The hardest thing she had ever had to do in her life.

"Marion would have drowned if not for you. Thank you..."

She hesitated, wondering what else to say and whether Tyler would accept a hug, wanting to touch her but not daring to. Tyler solved the problem for her when she reached for her sunglasses and slipped them on, putting a clear barrier in between them.

"No problem," she said.

She wanted to cry again and she had no idea why.

Very softly, Kate asked,

"How are you?"

Tyler looked at her and simply nodded. The gentleness in Kate's voice was unexpected, and just a little bit more of it would be enough to completely rip her composure apart. She was not prepared for it. Her mind went blank, and the only thing that she could think was that she did not want Kate to see her cry.

She was relieved when she spotted Marion walking out of the ambulance, with Ashley, still looking a little unsteady on her feet.

"Marion's being released," she said, forcing herself to smile. "Make sure she has something to eat, okay? I'll see you later."

Marion was tough and she did not stay down for long. After a good breakfast and a nap, she was back diving that very afternoon. She told Kate that she felt fine, albeit extremely foolish.

"Why?" Kate asked her that evening as they were going back to their hotel after a quiet dinner at a local restaurant.

"I should have made sure it was safe to go swimming in the first place. Instead of that, I almost drowned, and I almost took Tyler with me. Jesus."

Kate shivered a little at the thought. She had no answer to this.

Marion was right on both counts. She slipped an arm around her shoulders and pulled her close.

"Let's not think about that," she said.

"She always looks so sad, you know."

"Who does?"

"Your friend Tyler."

"She's not my friend."

Marion snorted. She stared at Kate, looking a little bit shocked.

"Oh no?" she said. "How do you call someone who saves my life?"

"I know. That came out all wrong, I'm sorry. I just mean... Tyler is..."

Kate stumbled on the words as she tried to explain what Tyler meant to her. In the end she simply gave up.

"Ty made it clear she didn't want to keep in touch after Staunton," she said. "What happened this morning doesn't change anything."

"Are you sure?"

"Yes."

"She keeps glancing your way when you are not looking, you know?"

Kate gave an impatient shrug. If only she had been alone with Marion in Sausset she would have adored every second of it.

The small fishing village was charming. It was hot, they were making really good progress with their diving. The food was to die for. Of course if she had been alone in Sausset her friend probably would have drowned that very morning.

She sighed in frustration.

It had been such a shock to arrive in Provence and find Tyler there. Then for a while all that Kate could feel was anger toward her.

Why did you leave? she wanted to shout. *I spent months worrying about you, wondering what on earth I could have done that made you want to disappear like that. I thought we had something, back there at Cobel. I thought it was more than just friendship. I know you felt it too. I miss you! Why did you run away?*

Marion glanced at her friend and noticed the sadness in her eyes.

"What did you say to her on that first day on the boat?" she asked softly.

"Not much. She said she could get us reassigned and I said great. I was angry. I know she wanted to talk, but..."

"But you told her to stay away?"

"Pretty much," Kate murmured, and she winced as she remembered the haunted look in Tyler's eyes.

That look she had hated so much at Cobel, now she was responsible for putting it in her eyes. Kate felt a little sick when she thought about it. Yet Tyler had done it, she had stayed away because Kate had asked her to.

All credits to her.

"She's with Ashley now, anyway. There is nothing to talk about."

Marion gave a low chuckle.

"How do you know she's with Ashley?"

"Please. It's obvious."

"It's obvious that they care a lot about each other, just like we do. But it doesn't mean we sleep together. And I don't get that vibe about them at all."

"Marion, can we talk about something else, please?" Kate said impatiently.

Marion stopped walking at the edge of the pier and glanced toward the catamaran moored at the end of the jetty. There was a single light on the bridge, and she nodded a little toward it.

"She'll be on there now," she remarked lightly.

"How do you know?"

"Tyler lives on that boat."

"She does? How do you know that?"

"I had a little talk with Ashley earlier. She came round to see how I was doing."

Kate sighed. She ought to have known this would happen. Marion could not leave things alone for a minute.

"Marion, can we not talk about this please?" she repeated.

"Ashley said Tyler isn't doing too good at the minute."

Kate tensed.

"What do you mean?" she asked, suddenly concerned. "What's wrong with her?"

"I mean that if you go there now, she will not send you packing. In fact I can promise you that. You need to talk to her, mate."

"And you got all that from a two minute chat?"

"It was slightly longer than that," Marion said.

She glanced at Kate and laughed a little at her expression.

"What?" she chuckled, her eyes shining with mirth.

Kate stared at her in amazement.

"Did you and Ashley..."

"Suffice to say I know for sure that she is not Tyler's partner," Marion interrupted, serious once more. "Get yourself on that boat and sort things out, Kate."

Kate took a deep breath and turned to observe the boat, her thoughts going back to Cobel and the moments she had shared with Tyler there. Front line stuff, she reminded herself carefully. When you might be dead in an hour, feelings and emotions were on the next level. Everything was more intense. She had felt very strongly about Tyler in Afghanistan. Unfortunately, she still did. Or maybe that was a good thing. She could not decide anymore.

Kate gave a frustrated sigh and she rolled her shoulders a couple of times.

Marion burst out laughing and pushed her forward.

"Go find her," she said.

Chapter Fifteen

Kate's heart was beating hard as she stepped on board and made her way toward the main cabin. It was just after nine. The harbour was quiet and the heat of the day had turned into just comfortable warmth. The boat was silent. She suddenly felt foolish creeping around like this. What if Tyler was not alone?

"Shit," she muttered under her breath.

She hesitated, almost turned around, then realised that she had to do this. She had to talk to her. If she did not, she would always wonder what if.

So she carried on up toward the upper deck, pausing when she heard the sound of guitar strings being softly strummed. She steadied herself and walked on toward the music, stopping when she spotted Tyler. She sat looking out at the islands of the Frioul in the distance, strumming a slow song that Kate did not recognise. But it was beautiful.

She was wearing her trademark blue jeans and a white flannel shirt, untucked and with the sleeves rolled up. She looked sexy and strong as she always did. And so desperately alone.

"Hey captain," Kate called softly.

Tyler turned her head and blinked when she saw her standing in the shadow of the bridge. Emotion sparkled in her eyes and she took a sharp breath.

"Hi," she said.

She immediately lowered her guitar down and stood up.

"What's the song?" Kate asked.

"Nothing... Just something I made up."

"It was really lovely."

Tyler nodded silently, observing Kate as she stood some distance in front of her. The ex-medic looked worried, uncertain. Tyler's heartbeat quickened.

"Are you okay? Is it Marion?"

"No, no. Everything's fine, don't worry," Kate reassured her quickly, realising that she should at least give her some kind of explanation for just showing up like that. "I just wanted to talk to you. You got a minute?"

"Sure. Hmm... Kate, I..."

Tyler stumbled on the words and her eyes filled with tears. For once she did not care whether or not Kate saw them.

"What? What is it?" Kate asked in alarm.

"I just hate this so much, you know?" Tyler whispered.

"What?" Kate asked softly, her heart beating wildly in anticipation.

She needed Tyler to take this forward now. She had made the first step, coming to the boat, and she needed Tyler to meet her halfway.

It was as if Tyler had read her mind.

"This," she said with feeling. "What happened between us... Not talking, pretending we don't know each other. I hate it, Kate. I don't want it, I never wanted that."

Kate started to cry, and she stepped forward to take Tyler in her arms roughly.

"I am so glad you said that," she exclaimed.

She started to laugh a little at the same time, and she gripped Tyler harder.

"I am so glad you said that," she repeated. "I kept trying to think what I could have done to piss you off, to make you want to leave like that..."

The comment and the intensity of the hurt in her voice hit Tyler hard in the centre of her chest.

"You didn't do anything Kate. It wasn't you. I am so sorry... I never wanted to hurt you."

Kate could feel her trembling in her arms. She pulled back a little, and brushed a tear off Tyler's cheek.

"Please don't get sad. Shall we sit down? Can we talk?"

"Yes, sure."

Tyler straddled the bench and sat facing her, her eyes sparkling in the low light reflected off the sea. Kate smiled at her and brushed fresh tears from her eyes.

Tyler was so close, and all Kate could think about was how much she wanted to kiss her. She could smell her. Fresh coconut shampoo and a hint of sun. She was assaulted by memories of how good her mouth had tasted that night, how soft her skin had felt. She was struggling to get her brain in gear.

"Gorgeous boat," she remarked.

"Thanks. I got it the first week I arrived here. It was in pretty bad shape but I put it back together."

A bit like me, Tyler thought.

"You did good. It's beautiful."

Tyler exhaled slowly. It was good to have Kate near her, talking to her, asking how she was and taking an interest in her. Her mind was clear and she felt centred. She realised suddenly that it was the first time in eight months when she had not felt like she was drowning.

"You know... When Marion said she wanted to go on this diving training thing in France, I thought it was a great idea. I was miles away from thinking that I would run into you here. And I know now that I wasn't ready for it. I'm sorry I acted like such a bitch to you Tyler."

"You didn't. And I don't want to be a problem for you."

"That's not what I said."

Tyler breathed deeply and hesitated.

"So what happened?" Kate said gently.

"Well. When Ashley heard that I'd been injured she came to see me at Staunton. She explained she was starting a business down here with Cathy, and she asked if I wanted in."

Tyler looked out toward the sea as she spoke, her luminous grey eyes sparkling as she remembered.

"Things were a bit crazy for me for a while, after Cobel, and I..."

"What do you mean, crazy?" Kate interrupted, immediately concerned.

"My leg didn't heal very well at first. And..."

Tyler hesitated again. Too much to get into just now, she realised. Better to keep it simple.

"I just needed to get away for a while," she said.

Kate nodded, her eyes on Tyler as she spoke. She knew she was not getting the whole story, but there would be time for that. For now all that mattered was that they were connected again. Tyler was back, she was talking and opening up to her once again. And Kate had never felt so happy. She had missed the sound of her voice, that husky, low voice she liked so much.

"I know I shouldn't have left like that," Tyler said. "And the longer I stayed away the harder it felt to reconnect."

This time Kate met her eyes and found it quite impossible to look away.

"I'm sorry," Tyler murmured.

"Hey, don't worry about it," Kate said gently. "You went through a lot. And also, it's not like we made a promise to hook up after Afghan."

"You did."

"What?"

"You did," Tyler repeated, smiling softly. "When I got injured, you said you would come for me."

Kate gave a little sad nod at the memory.

"Yeah. I was hoping that would give you an incentive not to die," she said, and she turned to give Tyler a crooked smile. "Looks like it worked. You were pretty out of it then, I wasn't sure that you had heard me."

"Oh, yes. I did."

Tyler did not tell her that Kate's promise had been the only thing which had kept her going after that last patrol. Through the long nights alone at Staunton when even huge doses of morphine would not ease the pain, and when she found out that she would have to leave the Marines. When Ben Collins' wife had screamed at her that she was to blame for her husband's death.

The only thing that had got Tyler through was the knowledge that Kate would come back for her one day. And now she really had.

"I heard you," she repeated.

Kate turned to her slowly. Her eyes looked beautiful in the fading evening light, and as she started to speak Tyler suddenly leaned forward and kissed her.

There was nothing slow, nothing unsure about that kiss. It was demanding, deep, searching, and it made Kate's blood sizzle and made her forget everything else she had wanted to say. Instinctively, she wrapped her arms around Tyler's neck. She let her hands drift up and down her back. She felt her breathe harder and she bit her lower lip to stop from crying out loud when Tyler's mouth drifted to her neck. Kate groaned.

"Tyler," she murmured.

And then, louder.

"Ty."

Tyler pulled back and looked at her as if she were in a daze. Kate held her breath as she took in the flash of heat in her cheeks, and the way her eyes burned. Tyler was breathing hard, and Kate could not quite believe how beautiful she was.

"You look dangerous," she observed.

"Sorry."

Kate gave a soft chuckle.

"Don't be. I like it," she said.

"I'm sorry," Tyler repeated as if she had not heard her.

She ran a hand through her hair and stood up to put some distance between her and Kate. She turned back to give her a flustered smile.

"You make me feel a little bit crazy," she admitted.

Forgetting her resolve to just sit and talk, Kate got up and went to stand in front of her, stepping even closer when Tyler took a step back.

Tyler leaned against the deck railing and put her hands on it to make sure that she would not touch Kate again.

"What are you doing?" she murmured as Kate pressed herself against her.

"What do you think I'm doing?"

Kate stopped just short of kissing Tyler again and waited. She stared into her eyes, saw desire raging inside, tempered only by the fear of doing something wrong.

"Are you sure?" Tyler asked quietly.

"No."

Kate started to undo the buttons on Tyler's shirt, one by one, very slowly. All the while Tyler kept her hands firmly on the railing, watching, worried that if she moved Kate might change her mind.

"At Cobel you wouldn't let me touch you," Kate murmured.

And she opened Tyler's shirt a little and lay her palm low on her stomach. She felt her take a sharp intake of breath, and looked up deep into limpid grey eyes.

"Are you going to ask me to stop now too?" she asked.

The look that Tyler gave her was so intensely sexual that it made her instantly aroused.

"No," she said huskily.

"Good."

"Come with me."

Tyler grabbed Kate's hand and led her down below deck to her bedroom. She shut the door and turned around, laughing when Kate just grabbed her and pushed her roughly down onto the bed.

"So I make you feel a little crazy, do I?" Kate asked as she straddled her lap.

She wrapped her arms around Tyler's neck and looked seriously at her.

"Yes. Amongst other things."

"What other things?"

Tyler rested her hands on Kate's hips, and looked up into the rich brown eyes of the woman she loved.

"Safe," she said softly.

Kate closed her eyes for a second.

Tyler's tone was casual, but her words meant so much to Kate.

"I make you feel safe?" she repeated, her voice betraying her feelings.

"Yeah," Tyler said.

Her voice had got a little bit huskier still, and her eyes were intense and hot. She lifted Kate's shirt a little, and let her fingers brush over her naked breast, watching her all the while. Kate bit her lower lip, tried not to react to Tyler's feather like touch. She wanted to take her time. But she was trembling already.

Tyler glanced at her, raised her head a little bit more, and blew gently on her nipples.

"Tease," Kate gasped.

"But you like it?" Tyler asked.

"Oh yes..."

Tyler smiled a little and closed her fingers around Kate's perfectly round breasts. She rubbed her cheek against them, breathed her in, and then she took a hard nipple in her mouth. A low moan escaped her as she closed her lips around it. She felt Kate's hands on the back of her neck, and Kate's fingers working their way up into her hair, making her head swim.

Kate sighed as she held Tyler against her.

"Take off your top," Tyler murmured.

Kate pulled the garment over her head quickly.

"You too," she demanded.

Tyler slipped out of her shirt and threw it across the room, and reached for the belt on Kate's jeans.

"Get rid of those too."

The jeans went flying across the room. Tyler pulled Kate back on top of her. She wrapped her arms around her waist, and she kissed her again, deeply, urgently. She was no longer playing, no longer teasing. She felt the way that Kate's hips moved up against her, asking for more. Tyler brought her head up, breathing hard. She traced a finger along the side of Kate's throat, between her breasts. She kissed her there, breathed deeply and closed her eyes.

"You know how often I wanted to do this when we were together at Cobel?" she said.

Kate shook her head no and looked down at her. She was finding it a little difficult to speak now.

"I wasn't sure you wanted me..." she murmured.

Tyler smiled a little, blinking back tears at the raw emotion contained in that simple little statement.

"I do want you, Kate," she whispered. "Let me make love to you."

It was darker in the cabin when Kate opened her eyes again. She was lying with her back resting against Tyler, cradled deep inside her embrace, feeling warm and completely spent.

She stirred a little and Tyler immediately tightened her hold on her.

She kissed the back of her neck, her eyes closed, smiling when she felt Kate stretch lazily against her.

"Hey doc," she murmured. "How're you doing?"

"Hmmm."

Kate raised herself up a little. She turned to face Tyler, and gave her a slow, happy smile.

"I'm doing great," she said. "How long have I been snoring?"

"Only about twenty minutes."

"I haven't felt this good in a very long time," Kate said, and she lay her fingers against the side of Tyler's neck and kissed her softly.

She felt her pulse going fast under her fingertips, and she smiled.

"Hey, is it me or are we rocking?" she asked.

Tyler laughed a little.

"Yeah, it's getting windy outside. You don't get sea sick, do you?"

"No. This is very nice, I like it."

Tyler tried not to tremble as Kate slowly caressed her breasts, then let her hand wander down the length of her stomach, over her hip and down the inside of her leg. She reached for the sock-like compression bandage that covered Tyler's injured leg, but Tyler stopped her immediately.

"Please don't," she said nervously.

Kate gave her a long look, spotted anxiety dancing in her eyes.

"Okay," she said gently. "I won't do anything you don't want me to."

Tyler nodded, and relaxed again immediately.

"Your skin is always so hot," Kate murmured. "I remember that from Cobel."

She kissed Tyler lazily, brushing her lips against hers. She smiled a little when Tyler went after the kiss impatiently, and she pulled back with a grin.

"Hey. Go slow," she said.

She carried on with her exploration, gently deepening the kiss. Once more she rested the palm of her hand against Tyler's stomach, enjoying the way that Tyler jerked and gasped as she did.

"Sensitive?"

"A bit," Tyler said.

"Good. Think I can make you feel hotter?" Kate whispered against her ear.

STRONG

"I don't know... takes a lot... Oh!"

Tyler held hard onto the side of the bed and could not quite prevent a small cry as Kate unexpectedly rubbed her hand between her legs and parted her.

"You were saying?" she asked, pleased and aroused by Tyler's reaction.

Tyler reached for her, sighing when Kate pushed her back down.

"Stay still, it's my time to play now," Kate murmured.

"I'm not very patient."

"That's okay. I will show you how."

Kate kissed the smile on Tyler's lips. She caressed between her legs again. Tyler arched her back, trembling in response.

"You are very easy to please..." Kate whispered.

"Yeah?"

"Hmm. Yeah."

"You don't like it?" Tyler said breathlessly.

"Oh, I do like it, captain. I love that I can make you feel like this."

She could feel herself getting aroused again, but this time she would not let Tyler touch her. This moment had been such a long time coming.

Kate could feel Tyler's body quivering beneath hers. Her eyes were hot and fastened onto Kate, tracking her every movement. Kate lay fully on top of her, pinning her arms back when Tyler tried to pull her down harder.

"No touching," she said. "You're not allowed."

The words alone were enough to make Tyler shiver. Her breathing got even faster when Kate dropped her thigh between her legs and started to rub.

"How do I make you feel now?" she asked.

"On fire..."

Tyler squeezed her eyes shut as Kate pressed her leg harder against her.

"Kate," she gasped.

"Easy. I don't want you coming just yet."

"I'm trying not to," Tyler said. "But I…"

"Yes, you can. I want to go slow. Do it for me."

Tyler tried to catch her breath as Kate sucked each of her nipples, taking her time. Her fingers were still firmly locked around Tyler's wrists. Her body was heavy and hot against hers, and her leg was pressed playfully against Tyler's centre, just enough to keep her on the edge

"Who's in charge now, captain?" Kate whispered against her ear.

Tyler shuddered all over.

"You," she whispered.

"And do you trust me?"

"Yes," Tyler replied immediately. "I love you Kate."

Her words were like a slice of light through Kate's heart. She glanced at her lover and saw desire so intense in her eyes it looked like pain. She lowered her head a little, buried her face against the side of Tyler's neck.

"Go now," she whispered, and she entered Tyler and stroked her hard at the same time.

Released at last, Tyler wrapped her arms around Kate and she closed down on her fingers. She held on to her as an orgasm so fierce it almost knocked her out blazed through her.

When she could see again she dropped back onto the bed, her hands shaking. She stared at the ceiling for a couple of minutes, feeling dazed, catching her breath.

"Jesus," she whispered eventually.

"No, it was all me," Kate said, her tone serious.

Tyler burst out laughing.

"What a relief," she said.

She turned her head to look at Kate, and chuckled a little when she saw the satisfied look in her dark eyes.

"Why the smug face?" she asked.

"Because," Kate said softly, "I got you to trust me."

"I've always trusted you."

"But tonight you let me see what's going on inside. Right here," she said, and she rested her fingers on Tyler's chest just above her heart.

She kissed her and pulled back until she could look straight into her eyes.

"Why did you run?" she asked.

Tyler tensed immediately. Kate saw in her eyes the impulse to pull away. To keep her distance again. If she had, Kate did not know what she would have done. She sensed the tremendous effort it took for Tyler to pull herself back into the conversation.

She did not run.

What she said made Kate's blood turn to ice.

"I had a girlfriend... A few years ago. She shot herself in the head with my service weapon."

Shock registered over Kate's face. She looked bewildered at first, and then her expression hardened, and she tightened her grip on Tyler's hand.

"What? Why? What happened?" she asked.

Tyler met her eyes and what she saw in them melted her heart. The love shining in Kate's eyes was so profound, her grip on her hand so strong. She looked ready to stand up for her and to fight for her, and Tyler had to look away, because otherwise she would have cried.

She took a deep breath, and started to talk.

"Her name was Helen," she said. "She was a lawyer for a big firm, worked a lot. She said she loved her job, and I know that it was true. But there was a lot of pressure with it as well. I didn't know it at the time, and she never told me, but she was struggling."

Tyler was looking through the round porthole on the side, far out across to sea as she spoke. It was easier that way. She had only told that story twice, to Collins and to Ashley. It was difficult to have to say it again, especially to Kate.

"She started drinking. A lot. Right about the same time that I started working more. I was away on exercise a lot, there was pre-deployment training, some missions I could not even tell her about. The usual stuff, but it's hard when you are on the outside and not involved. You know?"

Kate nodded her understanding, and gave Tyler an encouraging smile.

"I knew she liked her drink, but I never realised how much until she ended up in hospital after crashing her car, and I found a big stash of empty tequila bottles hidden in the yard. She got fired for drinking on the job. I found out she had a history of depression."

"What did you do?" Kate asked quietly.

Tyler shrugged a little.

She brushed Kate's cheek with her fingers, gave her a soft smile.

"There was nothing I could do," she said. "She dumped me. As soon as I started to question her drinking, she pushed me away. That was right before my first tour of Afghan, so I didn't have much of a choice, I had to leave her for six months anyway."

"Can't have been easy for you."

Tyler gave a bitter smile.

"Wasn't the happiest time of my life. She said we were over, but she kept on writing and emailing me. Just horrible stuff, blaming me for how she felt, saying that I should be at home with her, helping her." "Even though she had made it clear that she never wanted to see you again?"

"Yes."

Tyler shrugged a little, and tried again for a smile. But Kate could see how hard this was for her, and she held her tighter against her.

"You okay, honey?" she murmured.

Tyler nodded absently, her eyes a little bit glassy as she remembered.

"The day after I got back from Iraq I went for a run in the morning. When I got home I found that she had used her key to let herself into my place. She was drunk, and crying. She was sat on the kitchen floor holding my weapon in her hand. I never got round to changing the lock on my safe, and she still knew the combination..."

"Oh, Ty..."

"I tried to reason with her, but she could barely speak, and she certainly didn't want to listen. I think she must have been drinking for a while and she was in a bad state. I wish I'd managed to find the right words, to make her hear me..."

Tyler blew air out loudly. She seemed to get swallowed up inside the memory for a while. Kate had seen that look before. She recognised it from Cobel, when sometimes Tyler would get lost in thought for no obvious reason.

Now she knew what it meant. She kissed her softly on the lips.

"It's okay, darling," she said gently.

"She said it was all my fault, and that she hated me. I thought for a moment that she would try to shoot me."

Kate tensed.

"Did she threaten you?"

"Only when I tried to take the gun away from her. But then..."

Tyler did not finish her sentence but she did not have to.

Kate winced as she pictured the scene in her mind. She could not read the expression on Tyler's face, but she knew how she felt after hearing her story, and she could not get her head around how Tyler would have felt at the time.

She gently ran her fingers through her hair.

"I am so sorry, Ty," she said gently. "You know I am here for you, right?"

"I know."

"You don't have to say any more."

Tyler shook her head.

"No, I'm okay. I want to tell you. The thing is you see, even if I could have chosen to stay with her, I would not have done," she said, and her voice was tight. "Helen was right. I didn't love her more than my career, I wanted both. But I loved her so much," she added sadly. "I always loved her. And she didn't even know it."

Kate cupped her face in her hand. Tyler leaned into it and closed her eyes.

She sighed.

"So is this when you started to have panic attacks?" Kate asked.

"I had a few. There was an investigation into Helen's death. My previous relationships. I... I'm sorry Kate, I didn't want to get into all this stuff..."

"Why did you run?" Kate asked again, because she had to know.

"It doesn't matter now."

"Yes it does. Tyler, I love you, I would never hurt you. But you ran from me. You understand I need to know why?"

Tyler nodded a little.

"I understand. I just... I panicked, Kate. I thought I would let you down. I couldn't live with that."

"Let me down? How?"

Tyler shifted uneasily.

"I don't know," she murmured.

"You do not believe you are really responsible for your ex's suicide, do you?" Kate asked, watching her closely.

"Well. I did let her down, Kate. When she needed me. And Ben. I could let you down too."

Kate exhaled sharply. There it was at last, she thought. The naked truth. She could see from the look in Tyler's eyes that there would be no convincing her otherwise, at least not for the time being. No wonder she pushed herself so hard all the time, she reflected. No wonder connecting on a deeper level was such a scary thing for her to do.

Kate pulled her into a hard hug.

"I am strong inside, Ty," she said simply. "I want to be with you. But I will never compromise my own self in the process. So please don't worry about me. I know you, and I want you in my life."

Tyler nodded against her, and Kate frowned all of a sudden and pulled back.

"What do you mean about Ben?" she asked.

Tyler shrugged a little, her expression sombre.

"It was my fault," she muttered.

She shut her eyes tight but tears were falling down her face like a river now.

"How was it your fault, baby?" Kate asked quietly.

"I should have known!"

"And how could you have known that an older man taking his dead baby to the cemetery was going to blow himself up?"

"I should have searched him. I should have searched him and put him down."

Tyler hit the side of her injured leg with her fist, hard. She did it twice, and Kate grabbed her wrist before she could do it a third time.

"Don't," she said sharply. "Not ever."

She curled her fingers under Tyler's chin and turned her head until she could kiss her.

"I love you," she whispered. "Let me look at your leg."

Tyler brushed at the tears in her eyes. She looked away again.

"No. I can't..." she started.

"Sure you can. You can do anything you want to do, right?"

Tyler took a hard breath and shook her head no once more.

"I love you," Kate told her again with feeling. "You can do this."

After a few agonising seconds Tyler finally turned to her. She brushed at her eyes again and met her gaze.

She gave a shaky smile.

"I love you too," she said simply. "Have done for a long time."

"Then take that thing off your leg, Ty. I want you. And that means all of you."

Tyler hesitated. And then finally she made her decision and slowly started to remove the thick bandage that covered most of her left leg. Kate kept her hand firmly on her the whole time, gently kneading the knotted muscles in her shoulders.

Once the bandage had come off, Tyler looked at her leg quickly, then away, and she sighed.

"Okay," she said.

She sounded so defeated, so tired.

Kate kissed the side of her head, and squeezed her arm.

"It's all right," she said.

She ran her fingers slowly along the side of Tyler's thigh, over the thick scar in the shape of a U lower down her leg, just above where her knee would have been.

Tyler twitched and gave a surprised laugh.

"Wow. Feels weird."

"Weird how?"

"Weird as in… kind of nice."

Kate smiled at little.

"Fancy that eh," she said.

The scar looked just as she had expected it would. It was neat. Someone at Bastion had done a good job for Tyler. She took her hand and gently guided her fingers over the scar. She saw her wince a little.

"Feel it," she said. "It's all right. It's a part of you."

Tyler nodded silently.

"Does it hurt?"

"Not this bit."

"How does it feel?" Kate asked, looking at her intently.

"Okay. A bit funny. It's easier with you."

All of a sudden she felt more tired than she had in weeks. She shivered and rubbed her eyes, and Kate realised how much of a toll this conversation must have taken on her. She was proud of Tyler for being honest with her though, and also for facing her fears and allowing her inside.

"Time for bed now darling," she said gently.

Tyler let Kate push her down onto the bed and cover her with the light sheet. It felt like sinking into warm fluffy heaven. It was hard to keep her eyes open.

"Are you okay?" Kate asked.

"Hmm... Yeah. Kind of beat."

"Yeah, I can see that. Go to sleep."

"Are you going back to your hotel?" Tyler said drowsily. "Don't go, okay?"

"Don't worry about it, Tyler. I am not going anywhere, my love."

Kate slid under the cover and she pressed herself against Tyler's back, pulling the cover higher around her and resting her arm safely against her waist.

Tyler closed her eyes and exhaled softly.

"Kate?" she said.

"Yes, darling."

"I am very sorry. About everything."

"It's okay."

"Yeah. But I am sorry."

Kate wondered what she meant by that, but for now she knew they should just rest. There would be time to talk again, later, if they ever needed to.

"Don't worry, baby. Just relax."

Tyler nodded a little, and within seconds she sank into a deep, heavy sleep.

Chapter Sixteen

The next two weeks went by in a flash.

Over time, more and more of Kate's stuff started to appear on board Tyler's catamaran. It was easier that way since she was spending all of her free time with her anyway. The move happened quickly and naturally, without either of them feeling the need to discuss it. Tyler got a permanent smile on her face.

Every day they went for an early swim together followed by breakfast in the village with Marion and Ashley. In the afternoons if they were not diving they often took refuge inside the boat to escape the worst of the summer heat, and they spent hours alone below deck, making love, talking or simply relaxing in each other's arms.

Tyler took her lover to the university town of Aix-en-Provence, and they spent a day wandering the small streets and drinking coffee on the beautiful tree-lined Cours.

Kate fell in love with Cezanne and decided that she would like to learn how to paint. Tyler stopped complaining of phantom pain and her panic attacks seemed to stop altogether.

Kate did not comment on this, but she also noticed that Tyler became less and less concerned and self-conscious about her leg as the days passed. Gone was the sock that always covered it, and the blue jeans she wore even when it was too hot. When they were on the boat Tyler did not even bother with her prosthetic, which was uncomfortable in the heat, and she relied on her crutches, at ease with herself and using them.

She looked happy, and for the first time in her life she found that she was happy to slow down. There was nothing she felt she needed to achieve, nowhere she needed to go, nothing she had to prove to anyone. Just here and now had suddenly become enough, and life finally felt like it was worth living again.

On the morning after the last day of their dive training, Marion stood on the beach and proudly raised her glass of orange juice. She looked happily at her friends gathered around her on the sand, and grinned.

"To me and Kate, PADI qualified at last!" she said with a laugh.

"To you and Kate," Tyler and Ashley agreed in unison, raising their bottles.

"And to Ashley and Tyler, for being such fab instructors," Kate added.

Ashley slapped Tyler on the shoulder and winked at her.

"Fab. That's us, buddy," she said.

"And we have some news," Marion added as she sat down behind her girlfriend and threw her arms around her neck.

"What's that?" Kate enquired.

"I'm going back to York with Marion," Ashley announced with a beaming smile.

"So she can learn to speak English properly," Marion added with a quick wink at Kate. "Nothing else, of course."

"Of course," Kate said, laughing. "Ladies, that's wonderful news, congratulations."

"And you, mate, better learn to speak some French if you're going to be staying here with Ty."

"I'm giving her private lessons," Tyler said with a sparkle in her eyes.

"She any good?" Ashley asked.

Kate chuckled.

"I need lots of practice. Tyler doesn't mind."

She looked at Tyler, who sat on the sand wearing nothing but a pair of board shorts and a bikini top. Her prosthetic lay forgotten, half buried in the sand, and Kate could not remember ever seeing her girlfriend looking so relaxed.

When Ashley and Marion nipped for a quick dip in the sea she gave her a lazy kiss, smiling when Tyler pulled her down onto the sand with her.

"What are you doing?" she laughed.

"Nothing illegal," Tyler shot back, grinning. "We're in France, remember? We can do this."

As she spoke she softly ran her fingers over Kate's thigh. She kissed the side of her neck, and her hand wandered up and under Kate's silk shirt, pausing just underneath her breast.

"If you want to do something illegal," Kate remarked lazily, "I don't really mind."

Tyler's breath was hot against her ear as she smiled.

Kate turned her head a little until she could kiss her.

"You taste delicious," she murmured.

"I do?"

"Yep. I think I am going to keep you."

"Oh yeah?"

Kate smiled when she heard the delight in Tyler's voice.

"I am going to keep you," she repeated, seriously this time.

She sat up and pulled Tyler up with her.

"Would that be okay with you Ty?"

Tyler nodded, her grey eyes solemn as they travelled over Kate's beautiful face.

"Because if you say yes to that, I will never leave you. You know that, don't you," Kate said. "So you've got to be sure."

Tyler nodded slowly.

She held Kate's gaze, looked deep into her chocolate brown eyes, and bit on her lower lip thoughtfully when she saw how lovingly Kate was gazing at her. No one had ever looked at her that way before. And every single time that Tyler caught her girlfriend's eyes on her, whether it was on the boat, before a dive, first thing in the morning or last thing at night, it was always the same look. Loving, trusting, and strong.

Tyler gave her a smile and kissed her gently on the lips.

"I know that," she said. "And so, I hope you don't mind, but I got you a little something yesterday."

Almost shyly, she took a little black box out of her pocket and handed it to Kate. Inside was a simple heart pendant on a chain, and when Kate took it in her fingers and read the engraving on the back her eyes filled with tears.

It read:

'Yours Forever. I love you. Ty.'

Kate clutched the pendant in her hand and wrapped her arms around Tyler's neck.

"I love you so much," she said with emotion.

"Hey, that's good, but it wasn't meant to make you cry, doc."

Kate burst out laughing.

"I know! I'm not really. I just..."

"Just what?" Tyler asked gently.

"I just can't believe how happy I feel when I'm with you. Can you put it on for me please?"

"Sure."

Tyler fastened the pendant around her neck, and when she pulled back Kate was smiling at her. Tyler cupped her face in her hand and kissed her again.

"It's titanium," she said. "So it won't break. You can't lose it."

"I won't lose you."

"I know."

Tyler smiled.

"It looks good on you," she said.

Kate ran her hands through Tyler's thick, unruly strands of hair, and her eyes wandered to the beach around them. There was not a breath of wind, and the sun was hot. The sea was glittering a transparent blue, and a little distance away she could see Marion and

Ashley, walking hand in hand in the water.

Kate could smell the hills in the distance, hot pines and rosemary. Swallows were flying low in the sky.

She took a deep breath and closed her eyes.

"This is so perfect," she murmured.

The second she said that there was a shout from Ashley in the distance.

Kate shielded her eyes from the sun and gazed in her direction.

"Hey, you guys okay?" she shouted.

Ashley quickly jogged back to them. She had an urgent look on her face, and Tyler suddenly tensed up a little.

"What's up now," she muttered.

"Dave was just on the phone," Ashley said urgently when she got close. "We've got a shout."

"So what is going on? Are we talking about the entire East side of the hill? Or bigger?"

Kate listened to her lover's end of the conversation, not really liking the sound of it. She watched as Tyler strapped on her prosthetic, and continued to listen carefully to whoever was on the other end of the phone. She still had that energy about her, that vibrant, irresistible intensity which had so attracted Kate to her back at Cobel. Kate grew wistful as she remembered the gentle way that Tyler had made love to her the previous night.

She started to get worried.

"Okay, good. I'm on my way."

Tyler ended the call and stood up, turning to Kate.

"I've got to go."

"Just come here first please?"

Tyler walked up to her and Kate enfolded her in a tight hug. Tyler felt the tension in her body, understood that something was wrong in the way that Kate clung to her, as if she would never let go.

"Hey," she said softy. "What's the matter doc?"

She leaned into the embrace. Kate always touched her as if Tyler belonged to her. Tyler liked it. A lot.

"What does that guy want you to do?" Kate enquired.

On the way back to the boat, Tyler had explained that she and Ashley were members of the local Sea Rescue team. Dave was the guy in charge, and right now they were going out on a job. All of a sudden Kate had been reminded of Cobel.

"A fire started out in the hills behind Marseille early this morning, and the wind is making it worse," Tyler explained. "The fire fighters are worried that it could be coming our way."

Kate nodded and pulled back a little, feeling anxiety creep into her chest as Tyler spoke. It was the familiar feeling from back in Afghanistan. This dull, nagging worry that something nasty was going to happen.

She glanced toward the door as Ashley climbed on deck.

"So what does David want you to do exactly?" she asked again.

Tyler caught the anxiety in her voice, and she made sure to sound matter of fact when she replied.

"I'm driving up into the hills to warn the residents. I've done it a few times before. It's a bit of a boring job, but..."

"Can't you just phone them up?" Kate interrupted.

Tyler shook her head. Her voice was gentle when she spoke.

"Some of them don't even have electricity up there. That's how remote it is."

Kate grasped the front of Tyler's shirt and pulled her closer to her.

"Sounds dangerous, Ty," she remarked.

"It isn't."

Kate raised an eyebrow and stared deep into her lover's eyes.

"Trust me. It isn't," Tyler repeated.

"Is Ashley coming with you?"

"Yes."

Ashley was standing at the kitchen counter studying a map, and she raised her head slightly when she heard that.

She would be on the other side of the mountain warning the residents there. So, not technically with Tyler. She let it go, knowing this was simply routine and that there was no reason to worry Kate. The ex-medic was plenty worried already though, and she gave an impatient sigh.

"I don't know, Tyler, doesn't sound all that safe."

"Don't worry," Tyler insisted. "It's nothing much. I drive up, talk to the residents, make sure they are ready to evacuate if they have to. Then I drive back down. End of job."

"Okay..."

"They get fires quite often around here in the summer. This is nothing unusual, babe."

Kate relented. She did not really have a say in this, she knew it, and it was unfair of her to unload her anxiety onto her partner. She was just finding it impossibly difficult to control the rush of memories from Cobel, all of them bad, that the news of the fire had reawakened in her.

"Sorry," she said.

Tyler gave her a warm smile and pulled her into her arms again.

"Don't be. I like it that you care."

"Also, I sort of wanted you all to myself today."

"Same here," Tyler exclaimed, looking at Kate with a hungry look in her eyes. "All day, every day."

Kate laughed a little, and Tyler was glad to see the colour back in her cheeks.

"I'll be back by the time you finish today's dive. Fancy dinner in the village?"

"Absolutely."

Ashley grinned as the two women again got lost in each other's eyes.

"Great," she said, "how about I book a table for four?"

"Perfect," Tyler replied, her eyes firmly on Kate.

Her phone went off again and she grabbed it impatiently.

"Sorry. That'll be David again."

Kate nodded, and released her grip on her.

"Okay. I'll let you get on then. But please be careful."

Tyler gave her a wink and her familiar, trademark response.

"Always, doc."

A few hours later she stopped her jeep on top of a rise, and climbed out of the car into the baking Provençal afternoon sun. She was about ten kilometres from Sausset now, deep into the hills. She took a few steps away from the jeep, looking around and listening to the silence. It was dead quiet, worryingly so. The birds and all the cicadas all seemed to have gone away. Just like in Afghanistan, silence in those woods normally meant trouble.

Tyler dialled Ashley's number to give her an update on her progress.

"Are you on your way down yet?" Ashley asked immediately.

"Nearly. I've only got Annette's house to check out and then I'm done."

"The wind's just changed direction, Ty," Ashley informed her.

Her voice was tight, and she sounded worried.

"The whole of that area is under red alert now, and the fire teams are going up into it. You've got to get out."

Tyler's heart suddenly leapt in her chest, and she hurried back to the jeep.

"I can't believe it's changed so quickly," she exclaimed. "How long have I got?"

"Not long buddy. An hour at most."

"I've got to get to Annette's first."

"No. You've got to get out, Tyler. Leave it for the fire fighters."

Tyler gritted her teeth as a hole in the fire road threatened to

189

throw her car into the ditch. She was going hard now, driving a lot faster than she should have done. It would take the fire teams more than an hour to get to Annette's, she knew that. She gripped the wheel harder.

"I'm only a couple of miles away, I'm going to check her out," she insisted.

"Tyler, no. You know the rules."

"I'll pick her up and drive straight down the other side Ash, won't take me long."

Ashley sighed in annoyance and turned to look toward Marseille. She could see the smoke blowing their way over the sea, and the wind was strengthening.

"It's not looking good over here," she warned. "I'll say it again, Tyler. The fire is coming and it's a big one."

"Gotcha. I'll be quick I promise."

Tyler put the phone down and concentrated on the road. Her mood had shifted in an instant. Ashley rarely ever sounded worried, but this time she had. Tyler knew she had to take her warning seriously. She glanced at the phone again on the passenger seat and hesitated. She was dying to call Kate, but if she did she would probably just end up getting her worried over nothing. She sighed and returned her gaze to the narrow stretch of road in front of her.

Better not, she thought.

Every bump in the road was sending painful vibrations through her prosthetic and up her leg, and she was very glad when she came into view of the older woman's building. It was a very small stone house, barely bigger than a shepherd's shelter, and it looked in need of some work.

Tyler knew the woman who lived there quite well. Every once in a while she went up there for a chat and to bring her some food.

Annette was a local woman who after the death of her husband had decided to go live alone into the hills. Tyler liked her a lot. There was a time after Helen when she had thought she might disappear as well. She felt a strong kinship with Annette, and she was damned if she was going to turn around so close to her house and run away. Not letting her friend down ranked much higher than her own safety on Tyler's current list of priorities.

She parked her car right in front of the small dwelling and climbed out.

"Annette," she called. "It's Ty. Are you there?"

As she walked toward the back of the little house a couple of fire planes flew very low overhead, and Tyler felt apprehension snake its way down her spine.

The fire was coming all right.

She allowed her gaze to drift over the area of woodland and shook her head a little. Most other residents kept the space around their house spotless, clear of trees and scrubs, in accordance with fire safety regulations, but Annette did not bother with any of that. Her little house was right in the middle of a cluster of pine trees. If the fire swept across this area there was no way the little dwelling would survive, no matter what the fire planes and their incredibly gifted pilots would do.

Tyler had seen pictures of entire hilltops, devastated by fire, dotted here and there with little areas of colour. These were the houses that had survived. Little circles of life and safety. All courtesy of the French Canadairs. Their pilots were some of the best in the world. Yet even those guys would not be able to save this one, Tyler knew that for sure.

"Annette!" she yelled.

Her phone rang and she picked it up straight away.

"Ash."

"Ty. It's me."

Tyler stopped dead in her tracks at the sound of Kate's voice. It felt like an instant caress, cool and reassuring.

"Hey," she said. "Sorry Kate, I'm just running a bit late."

"I know, I just spoke to Ash. She's here," Kate said pointedly.

"Not with you as you told me she would be. Ring a bell?"

Tyler exhaled slowly.

"I know. Sorry. Didn't want to worry you."

"Yeah, well, whatever you wanted, you and I are going to have a little talk when you get back," Kate announced.

"About what?" Tyler asked suspiciously.

"About telling each other the truth, even when you think it'll make your life more difficult."

"Right. Okay."

"So have you found Annette yet?" Kate asked, her voice softening.

"Not yet."

Tyler was walking around as she spoke. She checked the small vegetable patch at the back, and found no one there. When she pushed the front door to the house it opened easily, and she stepped inside. There was a bed in the corner, a fireplace, a table and a chair.

The place felt empty and abandoned.

"This doesn't look right," she muttered. "I don't think she's here, you know."

"Okay. So you've done what you had to do, now leave."

Tyler stepped outside. She could smell smoke in the air now. The woods around her were still, and the sky had turned a hazy colour. Tyler glanced up at it, recognising the warning signs. She did not have long to get to safety now, and yet she hesitated. Her stomach clenched and tightened, and she experienced the same exhilarating rush of adrenaline she always used to feel before action in the field.

She breathed deeply, not entirely conscious that she was enjoying the feeling, and the clarity of mind that she always enjoyed in that particular instant. Danger always made everything so clear and sharp, and it left no time to think. It was easy. She welcomed it. Danger was close, and a big part of her was drawn to it, wanted to see it.

So she did what she should not. She lingered by the side of the car, scanning the woods as if daring the first flames to materialise in front of her. Playing.

"Tyler, can you hear me?"

Her lover's anxious voice cut through her dangerous daydream.

Tyler swore silently, and she got going again in a hurry. She would not tell Kate about this little moment, that was for sure.

"I'm here, doc. I'm on my way," she said firmly.

"Good! Listen, Ashley says to tell you to take the eastern road out. You got that? You know where you are going?"

"Yeah, I know the one. Ash is right, it's quicker that way. Listen, I'll call you once I am off the hills, okay Kate?"

"Call me before that. I mean it, Tyler. And be careful."

Tyler drove off, and she cursed under her breath as another bump in the road nearly jerked her off her seat. The phone flew out of her hand and landed on the floor. Without thinking she reached over to pick it up.

When she looked in front of her again, out of the dust, a small figure appeared in the middle of the badly maintained road.

"Shit!" Tyler exclaimed.

She hit the brakes hard and yanked the wheel to the right. On thick gravel, the car skidded off the road and onto the edge. Tyler had been going much too fast for it to stop there, and the momentum carried the heavy Jeep over the side. It rolled twice before slamming against a pine tree.

Tyler had not been wearing her seat belt, and the force of the impact sent her flying through the windscreen. She came down hard a few meters away from the vehicle. For an instant she thought she heard a voice calling out to her, before everything went black, and she lost consciousness.

Chapter Seventeen

Down by the water, Kate stood up and started pacing nervously in front of Tyler's boat, as Ashley tried once more to convince her that everything was fine.

It was nearly two o'clock in the afternoon. The entire village were out in the streets now, anxiously gazing up toward the hills, speaking on their mobiles and sharing out bits of news as the fire relentlessly burned its way toward them.

Every single member of the Sea Rescue team, fire fighters, and local volunteers were busy helping to evacuate houses around the area. Only Tyler was missing now.

"It's been an hour. I've served with her, and I can tell you that when Tyler says she will call, she does, no matter what. Something's wrong, Ash."

Ashley looked at Kate, then back in the general direction of the hills. She shook her head.

"Maybe. I don't know," she said somewhat uneasily.

"How long does it take to come down via that track normally?" Kate enquired.

"About an hour."

"So she should be here by now, or back on the phone."

"Yeah. That's unusual," Ashley admitted finally.

"We have to go look for her," Kate insisted.

"Kate, the fire is about to..." Marion started.

"I don't care about the bloody fire!" Kate exclaimed.

Her hands were shaking, and her voice broke.

"Bloody hell mate, Tyler is up there on her own and I know something has happened to her. I don't care about the stupid fire! I am going up, period!"

Marion bit her lower lip, her eyes full of tears as she stared at her friend.

"Sorry, Kate" she said quietly. "I am worried about her too. But the thought of you going up there at this point is even more frightening."

Kate wrapped her arms around her.

"I'm sorry honey," she said with feeling. "I didn't mean to shout at you. But I need to go get Ty. You understand, right?"

"Of course I do."

Marion nodded and immediately turned to Ashley.

"So, can we drive up?" she asked.

"You can stay here and be our liaison," Kate said quickly.

She raised a hand to stop her when Marion started to protest.

"I can't risk you getting hurt," she said. "This is my fight."

"Kate is right," Ashley said quickly.

She gave Marion a gentle smile and went to stand closer to her.

"I'll feel better and more able to concentrate if I know you're safe," she added.

Marion looked from one woman to the other, shaking her head in frustration, wondering if and when someone would try to stop being a hero for just a single sweet second. But for once in her life, and to her great credit, she did not protest. She took the phone Ashley gave her and clasped her hand.

"You look after yourself, okay?" she said. "Take a spare radio too. I'll find David and we'll be your backup down here. Be careful."

Ashley gave her a little salute, and Marion rolled her eyes.

"Always," her girlfriend said with a little grin then, giving her Tyler's standard reply.

The sky was a dusty orange haze now, and the smell of smoke was getting stronger. Kate filled a rucksack with bottles of water and a first aid kit. She grabbed a map from the back of Ashley's Jeep and stuffed it in her bag as well.

"Are you ready Ash?" she asked impatiently.

She watched as the woman gave Marion one last hug and jumped on to the seat next to her.

"We'll go up the Eastern road," Ashley informed her as she started to weave her way through the crowds out of Sausset.

"Okay," Kate said intently, staring straight ahead, not bothered which way they were going so long as they were. "Let's go, step on it."

Ashley glanced at her.

"Look, Kate, there is no guarantee that they will let us go up. You know that, right?"

"Who are you talking about?"

"The fire fighters. They'll all be up there right now."

"I don't care," Kate replied flatly. "I am going up on foot if I have to. I am not leaving Tyler."

Ashley returned her gaze to the road ahead.

"I'm glad you feel so strongly about her."

Kate stared at her profile for some time before she replied.

"I love her," she said in a firm voice. "I won't let anything happen to her."

"Good. Because she has been a hell of a mess, you know? She needs you."

"And you need Marion?"

Ashley smiled a little.

"It's that obvious uh?" she said.

Kate squeezed her leg and gave a soft chuckle.

"Yeah, it is that obvious," she said. "I'm glad you two found each other. Now floor it."

About the same time that Kate and Ashley left Sausset, Tyler came to in the middle of the woods. It took a second for her vision to clear, and when it did she stared at the small woman crouched down beside her.

"Bois un peu d'eau," Annette said, and she gently lifted a bottle of water to Tyler's lips.

Tyler tried to drink but she could only manage a sip before her stomach churned. She sat up, eyes squeezed shut, trying hard not to be sick.

"Annette," she muttered. "What the hell were you doing in the middle of the road?"

"Le feu," the woman said sharply, forcing Tyler to turn her head and look at her. "Y'a le feu, il faut descendre!" she said urgently.

She handed Tyler the prosthetic that she had lost on impact and waited for her to put it on. Tyler was pleased to see that the leg was intact. The Marines had done a good job providing her with the some of the very best in the industry. She was lucky.

She blinked when she felt something wet dripping into her eye, and brushed it away only to realise that it was blood. One glance at the car confirmed that it was totalled. She tried to get up and a huge ball of pain exploded between her eyes. The pain was so fierce it made her knees buckle, and she sank to the ground once more.

Annette was pulling on her arm, urging her to get up.

"Give me a minute," Tyler whispered.

"On a pas le temps," the little woman replied.

She was surprisingly strong for her age. She pulled Tyler to her feet, and rested her hands on her hips to stop her from falling.

"Respire," she said firmly.

"I am," Tyler muttered.

The pain in her head made her want to curl up on the ground and pass out. She realised she could still understand Annette's French though, and it made her smile a little. The petite woman took her face in her hands and waited until Tyler opened her eyes and looked at her.

"Tu es venue me chercher?" she asked gently.

"Yeah. I came to get you," Tyler said drunkenly. "Y'a le feu," she added in French, repeating what Annette had been telling her repeatedly for the past few minutes. There is a fire.

The little woman, who had very short white hair, tanned, leathery skin and bright blue eyes, smiled at her then. She kissed her on the cheek and pressed the bottle of water in her hand.

"Merci ma chérie," she said.

Then she wrapped her arm around Tyler's waist and pulled her forward with her.

"Viens," she added. "Je connais un chemin."

Kate and Ashley made it about half a mile up into the woods before they came across a fire truck. Immediately two of the crew stepped in front of their car and gestured for them to stop.

"Damn it!" Kate exclaimed.

"It's okay, I'll go talk to them."

Ashley jumped out and went to speak to the guy in charge, and when she ran back down to the Jeep Kate was already getting ready to walk.

"They won't let us through?" she said.

"No."

"I can't believe it!" Kate exclaimed, furious. "Have you told him we have a friend up there?"

"Yes, of course. But theirs is not a rescue mission at this point."

"This is so fucked up," Kate fumed. "But never mind. I'll walk."

She turned and rested a hand on Ashley's shoulder.

"You're not," she added.

"Don't tell me what to do," Ashley said evenly.

She reached into the car and grabbed her rucksack.

She started walking.

"Give Marion a call and tell her what we're doing," she said over her shoulder. "Let's go, doc."

Kate shook her head. She slammed the Jeep door shut and hurried after Ashley. So very much like Tyler, she thought. Oh God, I hope we find her.

Tyler went down on her hands and knees for the third time in ten minutes. She swore under her breath, and then gave herself a quick second to catch her breath and readjust her prosthetic. Ahead of her Annette was still going strong.

"Never thought I'd get dropped by a sixty-two year old," Tyler muttered.

Annette was wearing a skirt and a pair of espadrilles, and she was literally flying down the path. Where they were Tyler did not have a clue. Not on the path that Kate had told her to take, she knew that, and she was not entirely sure that this was a good thing. Her heart tightened at the thought of Kate, and it gave her the strength to get up once more. She could see that Annette had stopped and was waiting for her. Tyler caught up with her, and she was surprised when the woman gestured for her to sit down.

Too tired to ask why, she did as she was told, and she watched as the woman ripped the sleeves off her own shirt.

"Now what are you doing?" she asked drowsily.

"Tu saignes," Annette informed her, and she leaned forward a little to wrap the length of fabric around Tyler's head.

"Ah. Yeah, okay," Tyler said, and she leaned back a little. "Thanks..."

"Tyler," Annette called urgently.

She shook the younger woman until Tyler's eyes snapped open again.

"Sorry," Tyler sighed. "I'm a bit slow just now."

She coughed. There was a lot of smoke in the air now. She wondered if they were going the right way, away from the fire, and if it was simply catching up with them.

She looked at Annette and saw deep worry reflected in her eyes. Smiling gently, she reached out for her and squeezed her arm.

"Hey, don't worry," she said. "We'll be fine."

"I think we're lost," Annette blurted out.

Tyler stared at her, eyes wide.

"You speak English?" she said.

Annette burst out laughing.

"Un peu," she admitted shyly.

"Un peu, right?" Tyler repeated with a grin of her own.

She allowed herself to rest for a little while longer. How much worse could it get, she thought. So now on top of everything they were lost.

"Désolée," Annette said softly.

Tyler smiled at her, determined to keep them thinking positive. She had noticed that Annette looked a bit pale now, and genuinely frightened. She could not afford to follow her down that road or they would both be toast, literally. She had done a lot harder things in the Marines on training, and she been in a lot more nasty situations on countless operations.

She knew she could beat this one hands down.

"Don't worry, it's fine," she repeated. "We're going to find a way out, I just know it."

She examined the terrain all around them. Typical Provencal landscape, she reflected. White rocks in the distance, and miles and miles of garrigue in between. Brambles and bushes, rosemary, thyme, pine trees. Perfect kindling, she realised grimly. The air was hot and smoky, and the pain in her head seemed to be getting worse. Not looking so good, she thought privately.

Once again she found herself drifting. If Annette has not grabbed her and pulled her up she probably would have gone to sleep right there.

"Don't let me sit down again," Tyler said firmly.

Kate's throat was aching from yelling out Tyler's name over and over. Both she and Ashley had tied wet scarves to the back of their necks and pulled them up and over their mouth and nose. Ashley was doing the navigating, and she was keeping them going back and forth across the fire road that Tyler would have been on. Should have been on. They searched every inch of the woods on both sides of it as they made their way slowly up the hill, and still they could not find any sign of her.

It had taken them a long time to make it up to Annette's house, and that was when they had found the Jeep. Before Ashley could tell her to be careful, Kate had jumped straight down the hill, rolled a few times, and come to a stop against the car.

Tyler's mobile phone was abandoned on the floor and the vehicle was empty.

"Where is she?" Kate had cried desperately, out of breath with fear and anguish. "Damn it Ash, there's blood all over this thing!"

"Look, if she's not here, it's a good sign," Ashley had reminded her calmly. "Okay? Means she's walking and on her way down. Now we just have to find her. Can't be that far."

Two hours later and they were still searching.

"What's Marion saying?" Ashley asked as they paused for a minute.

She had to squint to see Kate through the heavy dust surrounding them. This was hard going, and she could not understand why they had not found Tyler yet.

Ashley had to believe that she would have headed down away from the direction the fire was coming from, but she caught herself wondering if they might be wrong thinking that. Although she had total faith in her friend's abilities, she knew that if she was injured, Tyler might not be thinking straight.

She kept her thoughts to herself, knowing how worried Kate

already was. They just had to keep going.

"The fire is still being held off on the other side of the hill," Kate told her. "For how long I don't know. David is at the harbour with Marion."

"Good, I'm glad he's with her."

"He's trying to round up some more people to help us with the search, but they are still busy evacuating as well."

Kate scanned the woods around them and hated being here with a vengeance. She hated knowing that Tyler was lost somewhere in this wilderness, and that she was unable to get to her.

"Let's go," she said tersely, and started going down again.

"Hang on, Kate," Ashley said.

"What?"

"Shh…"

Ashley stood with her head cocked to the side, listening intently.

"Did you hear that?" she asked.

Kate froze in place.

"I can't hear anything…"

"Just listen for a second," Ashley insisted.

At first all that Kate could hear was the roar of the wind burning through the trees. Then she focused on something else that sounded a whole lot more promising.

"Whistle?" she ventured.

"Yes!" Ashley beamed. "This way! Let's go!"

They went crashing through the woods, running now. A couple of times they stopped, and the whistle kept on going. Please let it be her, Kate was praying as she ran. Please, please let her be okay.

They ran down about a mile and a half through ankle breaking terrain, and then Ashley stopped and pointed at something in the distance.

"I think it's them!" she exclaimed. "Gotta be. Come on!"

The look of relief on Annette's face when they finally caught up with her was indescribable. She grabbed Ashley and immediately started chatting to her in excited French. This made absolutely no sense to Kate, and she still could not see Tyler.

"Ash, where the hell is Ty?" she shouted.

She looked wildly around her until she spotted her lover a little way behind, covered in blood, and limping slowly toward them.

"Jesus," she exclaimed. "Tyler!"

She ran toward her, almost falling over in her haste to get to her.

"Hey doc," Tyler said as Kate finally reached her.

She looked exhausted, but she forced a smile when she spotted the fearful look in Kate's deep brown eyes.

"Don't worry, I'm okay," she said quickly.

Kate immediately wrapped her arms around her.

"You don't look it."

She hugged her fiercely.

"Sit down so I can have a look at you," she advised.

Tyler did not have to be told twice. She knew they should keep moving, but the temptation to stop and rest was overwhelming. She tried not to let it show though, and she did her best to hide how bad she was actually feeling.

"Sorry, we got a little lost," she sighed. "Did you hear me whistle?"

Kate smiled a little as she used her wet scarf to wipe some of the blood off Tyler's face.

"Yes. Good lungs. Makes up for leaving your phone in the car I suppose."

"Ah, yeah... Guess I wasn't thinking properly."

"Weren't you? Why not? Did you hit your head?"

"Uh... yeah."

"Lost consciousness?"

Tyler hesitated, and Kate shot her a warning look.

"The truth, and nothing but the truth, captain. So?"

Tyler had no choice but to come clean.

"I did, but it was only for a few seconds."

"All right."

Kate glanced toward Ashley, who was looking after Annette and giving her a little food and water. Surprisingly, the older woman looked extremely well after their ordeal. Tyler did not.

She was covered in dust and bleeding, and despite her lover's attempts at reassuring her, Kate was genuinely worried about her. She carefully peeled Annette's improvised bandage off her head, wincing at the size of the cut just below her hairline.

It was deep, and it looked serious.

"Bloody hell, Tyler," she murmured. "It's a wonder you managed to make it down this far."

"I've got Annette to thank for that. How is she doing?"

"Doing well Ty, don't worry," Ashley informed her from behind.

Kate reached into her bag for some disinfectant and some gauze. She cleaned Tyler's wound as best she could and wrapped a clean bandage around her head.

"You'll need stitches but this will do for now. Can you see me okay?" she asked.

Tyler shrugged a little.

"Yeah," she said, although her eyes were burning and her vision was a little blurred.

She figured telling Kate about it would not change how she felt, so there was no need to share the information.

"Does anything else hurt?"

"No, I'm good," Tyler assured her.

Kate gave an impatient shake of the head. She had a pretty good idea how Tyler really felt at this precise moment, and good was definitely not one of the options.

She pulled her against her and wrapped her arms around her safely.

"You know you don't have to pretend when you're with me,

right?"

In spite of herself Tyler closed her eyes and let herself rest against Kate.

"I know, doc..." she murmured.

Ashley squatted down next to them.

"How are things with Ty?" she enquired.

"Concussed, I think, although she won't admit to it. We need help getting out of here, Ash."

"Already took care of it. I spoke to David and he is going to get the Rescue helicopter to come get us."

"When?"

"Just waiting for an update on ETA right now."

"How many can they take?"

"It's a Sea King. They'll take all of us."

Kate stared at the horizon. She could not see any flames yet, but the sky was hot all around them. She looked down at Tyler and gently cradled her head against her shoulder.

"Won't be long now sweetheart," she whispered softly to her.

Tyler was lost in thoughts of another time, when another helicopter had come for her. She reached for Kate.

"I don't like helicopters," she murmured.

Her eyes were still closed but Kate could see the tension in her face.

"Hey, Ty, look at me for a second," she said.

Tyler blinked a few times and focused on her face.

"Hi," she croaked.

Kate rested a gentle hand on her cheek and smiled at her.

"I know what you're thinking honey, but this is different this time, okay? I am coming with you. Nothing bad is going to happen. Just hang in there."

Tyler nodded slowly, and her eyes closed again.

"I know... Just memories," she sighed.

Just then Ashley tapped Kate on the shoulder and passed her the phone.

"Marion wants to talk to you," she said.

Kate turned around and grabbed the mobile.

"Hi mate," she said.

"Hi, how are you?"

"I am going to be so happy when we get off this stupid hill," Kate exclaimed, her voice heavy with sudden fatigue.

"I know," Marion said with feeling. "Are you okay? Ash tells me Tyler looks like the lead in a horror movie."

Kate rolled her eyes, and Ashley gave a soft laugh and a guilty shrug.

"Marines humour. Just trying to keep her spirits up I think," Kate remarked. "Any news on the chopper?"

Ashley glanced at Kate at that instant, and she frowned when she saw the stricken look on her face.

"What?" she asked, immediately on the alert.

Kate shook her head, listening intently.

When she put the phone down her expression was sombre.

"What's going on?" Ashley repeated impatiently.

"The helo's not coming."

"What? Why not?"

"It's not safe enough to fly. Kind of makes sense, really."

Ashley swore a few times.

"Damn it," she exclaimed. "It's going to take us a couple of hours at least!"

"I know. So we better get going, right?"

Ashley gave a tight nod and went to speak to Annette, whilst Kate gently shook Tyler awake.

"I've got news," she said.

"Let me guess, we're on our own," Tyler pre-empted her.

"Afraid so. It's too dangerous to fly in for them now, and for us, so we are going to have to walk."

Tyler rubbed her face with both hands and stared up at the sky.

"Sure, why not," she muttered. "I can walk. No problem."

"How is your head?"

"I could do with being in a cool dark room right now. But never mind."

"I know. I'll get you there soon. Want to wear my sunglasses? Might help a little."

Tyler let Kate pull her up and slipped on her sunglasses.

"Hey, doc."

"Yes?"

"I'm sorry I got you into this mess."

Kate narrowed her eyes at her. This sounded a lot like the conversation they had had once before. Tyler blaming herself for events way beyond her control.

Kate threw her arms around her and hugged her hard.

"I wanted to come get you," she said. "Now I am taking you home. Nothing else. Nothing you wouldn't do for me. Okay? No big deal."

Tyler buried her face against the side of her neck.

"Okay. I love you," she murmured.

"I love you too, babe."

Kate let her go, albeit very reluctantly.

"Let's do this thing, captain," she said firmly. "You owe me dinner in town, so let's get cracking."

"Ready to go, ladies?" Ashley asked.

Her eyes were on the horizon, and she looked worried. Kate resisted the urge to look back at the darkening skies and the huge columns of smoke that seemed to be getting closer all the time.

"I'll race you home," Tyler declared.

Annette went first, followed by Ashley. Tyler slotted in right behind her friend, and Kate went last, to be able to keep an eye on her partner.

They started at a fast pace, and once they got going no one turned back. Heads down, they ploughed on, through the increasing heat and gathering smoke.

After a while, despite the conditions, despite her head, and despite her prosthetic, Tyler naturally fell into a rhythm. She vaguely registered when hot ash started to rain down on them, but she did not dare slow down. Only once did she turn around to look back at Kate, and gestured for her to catch up.

"Stay beside me, okay?" she said. "I don't want to lose you in all this clag."

Kate nodded and she took her hand, and they both pressed on.

Tyler had been there before, with the Marines. On never ending training exercises, in the mountains, through the desert. She knew that pain, that point well beyond exhaustion, when you just had to put your head down, and keep going. She could do that. With Kate by her side, she could easily walk a hundred miles through the fire if she had to.

It took them three long hours to get off the hills, and by the time they made it back to the road the fire had once more shifted direction. It looked like they were in the clear.

"You guys wait here, I'll go get the car," Ashley commanded.

"Je viens avec toi," Annette said immediately.

Tyler opened her mouth to speak, but Kate pulled her firmly to the side.

"You and I are going to take it slow, okay?"

"If I sit down now I won't be able to get up again Kate," Tyler said tiredly.

"Would it be such a bad thing?"

"Yeah. Can't quit now."

"Right. Is it a marines thing, this annoying stubbornness?"

"I think it's just a me thing," Tyler said after a second's hesitation. Kate chuckled.

She remained by Tyler's side as they slowly walked up the hill a little way behind Ashley and Annette. After a while Tyler started to laugh. She leaned against her lover, still standing up, laughing as blood slowly trickled down the side of her face. Kate wrapped her arm around her shoulders and she frowned.

"What's so funny?" she enquired, puzzled.

Tyler squeezed her eyes shut, and rested her hand flat on top of her head.

"Damn," she giggled a little drunkenly, wincing. "Hurts when I laugh..."

Kate reached for her and kissed her on the lips gently.

"You fool. Of course it does."

Tyler took a slow breath and started walking again.

"It's better when you kiss me..."

"Good. So what's so funny?"

"I just thought about the last time I felt as tired as this, and it was with Ashley..."

Tyler stopped abruptly and grinned at Kate.

"With Ashley?"

"Yeah..."

Kate raised a wary eyebrow.

"Were you two... ever together?"

Tyler shook her head a little, her eyes on her friend in the distance. A smile tugged at the corners of her lips as she remembered.

"Once, almost," she said. "The whole thing was a bit clumsy."

"Clumsy how?"

Tyler started laughing again softly.

"We'd been on a training exercise for a few days. It was the sort where they dump you in the mountains and all you do is crawl around in mud, freeze to death at night, and do a lot of running around in circles."

Kate snorted.

"Yep, I know the kind. Can't say I miss them much. Can you

walk and talk?"

"Yeah."

"Good. So what happened?"

"On the day we finished the exercise, Ashley was supposed to get back to San Francisco but she missed her bus. So I invited her to spend the night at my house."

Kate rolled her eyes.

"Okay, I can see where this is going. I don't think I need all the details, Ty."

Tyler smiled and brushed blood off her cheek.

"It's a funny story. You want to hear?"

Kate was curious despite the little buzz of jealousy she felt. And she was keen to keep Tyler's mind off her injured head. She wrapped her arm around her partner's waist and let her lean against her as they walked.

"Go on," she said with a little smile.

"Okay. So we were both really, really tired. We had a shower, separately, and then we sat on the couch and Ashley had a couple of beers. And then she kissed me. Dropped her bottle and spilled half her beer down the back of my neck."

Tyler laughed at the memory, stopping again.

Kate nudged her on gently.

"Nearly there. Keep going."

"We had known about each other being gay for a long time, so that was okay. And then Ashley said perhaps we'd better just 'do it' once, just to see if we were right for each other. So I said fine."

Kate glanced at her partner, laughing in spite of herself.

"Right," she said. "Very romantic."

Tyler stumbled, almost drunk with fatigue now, but she kept going.

"Every time Ashley tried to kiss me I just couldn't help but laugh. After a while Ash got the hump with me and stormed off to bed."

Kate looked at her as Tyler slowed.

"What happened next?" she asked.

"I went to bed with her."

"And?" Kate insisted.

"Nothing," Tyler replied with a little smile. "We tried... But Ash is like my sister. In the end we just fell asleep and that was that."

She stumbled again, and it was obvious that she would not be able to keep going for long.

"How far are we now, Kate?" she murmured.

"Not far. You're doing great, honey."

Tyler took a hard breath.

"I think I'm going to throw up. I am so tired, this isn't even funny anymore."

"Was it ever?" Kate muttered.

CONCLUSION

Annette was released from hospital almost immediately, and announced that she was taking a taxi to go spend some time with her nephew in Toulon. She insisted on seeing Tyler first, who sat on a treatment table waiting for Kate, still covered in blood and dust and looking exhausted. Annette simply put her arms around her, cupped her chin in her hand and whispered a few words to her that made Tyler chuckle. Then she gave her a big smack on the lips and walked away smiling.

"Hello captain."

Tyler's eyes lit up when she spotted Kate watching her from the doorway.

"Hello doc."

"Snogging the locals I see?"

Tyler gave a tired smile.

"No energy left for any of that I'm afraid."

Kate walked to her and stood in between her legs close to the exam table. Her expression was serious, and remained so even when Tyler rested her hands on her hips and pulled her closer to her. She lay a cool hand on her forehead, and then gently brushed the hair from her face.

"You're burning up," she remarked with a frown. "How are you feeling, really?"

"I'm okay," Tyler said.

She shivered a little, and Kate rolled her eyes.

"Must be a glitch in your programming," she muttered.

"What?"

"Always lying to me about how you feel."

Tyler watched as she snapped on a pair of latex gloves and grabbed a suture kit.

"What are you doing?" she asked.

Kate gave her a stern look and a crooked smile.

"Do you really think I am going to let some strange doctor put his hands on you?"

Tyler relaxed immediately.

"Good. I hate doctors," she declared.

Kate pulled a stool in front of her and chuckled softly.

"No you don't," she said. "I am one of them, remember?"

They were eye to eye now. Tyler rested her clear grey eyes on her, and Kate felt her heart tighten. The urge to protect her, to take care of her, was absolutely overwhelming. She briefly touched her lips with hers, and then pushed her down gently.

"Relax, honey."

"I do love you," Tyler said.

Kate smiled as she reached for an alcohol swab.

"Good. And I am sorry, this is going to sting a little," she said gently.

"Go for it."

"The MRI didn't show anything we need to worry about, Ty," Kate explained as she worked. "Collins was right, you do have a pretty hard head..."

"If I recall, he said that about you, doc, not me," Tyler pointed out.

But Kate had spotted the instant flash of emotion in her eyes at the mention of her friend, and she immediately reached out to touch her hand.

"I miss him," Tyler murmured. "When we were at Cobel, he wanted me to kiss you. Did you know that? Kept telling me I should make the first move."

Kate gave a soft laugh and carried on with her work.

"Really? I had no idea."

214

"He would be happy for us now," Tyler reflected, and she raised her hand to her head.

"Hey, don't touch it," Kate warned, taking her hand and lacing her fingers through hers instead.

"Right. So can we go home now?"

"I don't know about that. One night in hospital wouldn't hurt."

Tyler tried to sit up and felt instantly dizzy.

"See?" Kate insisted. "You should stay. You can barely open your eyes, and I have just put seven stitches in your head."

Tyler gave her a pleading look and managed to sit up this time.

"No," she said more firmly. "I hate hospitals. I feel like shit. I want a shower, and I want my bed."

"I don't like seeing you in hospital either," Kate conceded. "But..."

Tyler gave her a little look.

"I want you in my bed too, doc," she said.

Kate gave a low chuckle.

"Well. Now you're talking," she said.

It was just getting dark by the time they made it back to Sausset, and Tyler was glad of the fact. She was hurting. Despite the big dose of pain killers Kate had given her at the hospital she had a major headache, and it only seemed to be getting more intense with every step that she took.

She had a quick shower, picked at her food, and went to bed wearing her favourite oversized USMC hoody. She snuggled deep under the covers as Kate busied herself with bandages and pain killers. Tyler watched her intently the whole time. It was wonderful to have her moving around the room, she reflected. Not to be alone. She smiled a little and took her time stretching.

"How do you feel?" Kate asked her for the third time in just about ten minutes.

Tyler thought for a second.

"You know that feeling when you go for a long hard swim, and then dress up in warm clothes and drink hot chocolate?" she said.

Kate paused to consider this for a moment.

"Yeah I think I know what you mean," she smiled. "If I replace your swimming with rowing in the cold for hours. Endorphins kicking in. I call it my 'Zen feeling'."

"Yeah. That's how I feel," Tyler said with a little grin. "'Zen feeling. That's cool, I like it."

She gave her lover a mushy smile and sank deeper onto the bed.

"I feel delicious. Are you coming in?"

"Soon. I just want to call Ash first, make sure she and Marion got back okay."

"Okay. Tell them I said hi."

Kate went up the stairs to call, and when she got back Tyler was fast asleep already. She had pulled the covers tighter around her. She lay on her stomach across the bed, the hood of her sweater pulled loosely over her head. Kate moved carefully next to her, sliding close under the covers but mindful not to wake her. She lay a soft hand on her cheek, and frowned a little when she realised how hot her skin still felt.

With a sigh she settled next to her, and she allowed herself to rest her hand on her arm. The touch grounded her, reassured her that Tyler was there, back in her world once more. Connected, forever at last. She closed her eyes and breathed out. Within minutes she was asleep too.

Kate woke up a couple of hours later when a scream shattered the silence. She bolted upright and reached for Tyler, who was kneeling up facing the wall, and punching it with all her might.

"Stop! What are you doing!" Kate exclaimed.

She grabbed Tyler's wrist to stop her hitting the wall again, and she gasped at the look of panic she saw in her eyes.

"Ty, it's okay," she said quickly.

Tyler was staring wildly at a spot behind her head and twisting to get away from her.

"Don't," she yelled.

"Tyler, it's me. Come on, wake up."

She was covered in sweat and crying.

The look of fear in her eyes scared Kate half to death. Quickly, she put her arms around her and tried to get her to calm down.

"It's okay, it's okay… I'm here," she murmured.

Tyler struggled against her still, and Kate rested her hand against the back of her head, holding her close.

"Just breathe," she said gently. "It's only me, babe."

"Kate?" Tyler mumbled.

"I'm here. You had a bad dream. It's all right, I've got you."

Tyler trembled in her arms.

"They'll cut me," she whispered, and she started to hyperventilate again as the old panic grabbed hold of her once more.

The dream was pulling her back under. She was back in that room, back in Bastion before the op. She had regained consciousness just as the surgeon was marking her leg. She had tried to argue with him, to stop him, but all he kept saying was that she would not feel a thing, and that they would make her sleep now, and not to worry. She was scared to death of going to sleep and not waking up. She had struggled. She remembered how he had nodded to a couple of nurses then. Suddenly there were hands grabbing her, holding her down. Someone had forced an oxygen mask over her face. In her dream the woman holding the mask was always Helen.

"No," she sobbed.

Kate closed her eyes and held her harder.

"I'm here, baby," she said firmly. "I am not leaving you and nobody is going to hurt you. I promise."

Tyler shook her head and struggled against the memories.

"Relax. It's just me and you now," Kate told her.

She settled more heavily against Tyler.

She held her for a long time, just rocking gently, whispering to her, and after a while Tyler finally settled down. The night was still and warm and the boat was rocking gently as it always did. Kate's arms were strong around her. Kate was holding her. This was real. Not the other stuff.

She took several shaky breaths and allowed her lover to pull her back down against the pillows. Tyler burrowed against her and she shivered.

"I'm sorry," she muttered.

"Don't be," Kate said immediately. "You get that dream often?"

Tyler nodded a little and pressed herself tighter into her lover's embrace.

"How often, sweetheart?"

"I used to get it three or four times a week."

"Used to?"

"Yeah. I don't get it when you're around."

Kate closed her eyes.

"And the panic attacks?"

"Same thing," Tyler said softly. Then she added, "I don't want to go back to sleep."

Kate kissed the top of her head and nodded.

"Tell you what, me either. Want to go get some fresh air?"

"Yes."

They sat on deck under the stars, legs dangling over the side, drinking ice tea. Kate pulled the zip on Tyler's fleece a bit higher, and she framed her face in her hands, looking at her intently.

"You okay? Are you warm enough?" she asked.

"Yes, thanks. Sorry about the..."

Kate raised her hand and gave a small shake of the head at the same time.

"You really have nothing to be sorry about," she said.

She glanced at Tyler's hand and sighed at the sight of the already swollen and bruised knuckles.

"You need some ice on that," she said.

"Yeah," Tyler said, so softly that Kate barely heard her.

"I'm glad you hit the wall and not me," she joked, and she nudged

Tyler's shoulder playfully, smiling as she did.

Tyler shook her head.

"I hate this," she said darkly. "I could have hurt you."

"But you didn't," Kate interrupted firmly. "And I am just worried about you. PTSD is not something to be taken lightly."

Tyler turned to her with tears in her eyes.

She looked a little shocked.

"I didn't want you to know" she said. "How did you..."

"I'm a doctor, Ty. I know the signs. And I know you."

Somehow Kate had known for a long time that Tyler was affected. She knew it about her when they were at Cobel. She had assumed then that it was linked to some event in her past.

When Tyler had told her about her lover's suicide she had realised that it had probably been the trigger, and obviously the events at Cobel would only have made it worse. Now the fire, the crash, and the long march through burning woods could easily have brought it all back.

"There is nothing wrong with me, Kate," Tyler said stubbornly.

"I know that babe. You had a stressful day that's all."

"My left ankle is driving me nuts."

"Phantom pain," Kate acknowledged. "Feels very real, doesn't it?"

"Yes, it does," Tyler agreed with a small nod.

Kate pursed her lips, feeling frustrated at the thought that she would never really be able to help with this kind of pain. She was silent for a little while, and then she spoke again.

"Sometimes I dream about Cobel too," she said softly.

"Bad dreams?" Tyler asked immediately.

When Kate nodded silently she tightened her hold on her hand.

"What sort of dreams?" she asked.

"Mainly ones in which I can't stop someone from bleeding to death."

Kate smiled sadly as she looked at her lover.

"You're in those dreams sometimes. I lose you in my dreams, and today I almost lost you for real. Third time now, Tyler."

Tyler returned her stare, and her eyes were calm now, and true.

"There won't be another one," she said. "I promise."

"Say that again."

"I promise, Kate."

Kate smiled a little, and kissed her softly on the lips.

"Okay," she said. "I believe you."

"What was it like for you after I got medivaced out?"

Kate took a deep breath.

"It was very chaotic for a while," she said. "The guys were wild, angry. You were gone, and so was Ben. Everything felt very out of control, and for a while it really was. It was the scariest situation I have ever been involved in."

"But the company commander was there, right?" Tyler asked, frowning a little.

"Yes, but it didn't really help. The guys needed one of their own. It was Lenster who saved the day in the end. He took charge, he talked to everyone. He was amazing."

Tyler nodded, looking pleased and not surprised.

"Lenster is a good guy. Solid. The more stressful things get, the better he normally performs," she remarked.

She nodded at Kate, her clear grey eyes glistening softly in the moonlight as they settled on her face.

"What about you, what was it like for you after I went?"

"Horrible."

Kate didn't have to think about that one for very long.

"It was awful," she said with feeling." We went back to camp, and I went back to our tent, and all your stuff was there. But you were gone. It felt like a bad dream. I couldn't believe I didn't jump on that helicopter with you when I had the chance. If it was now, I wouldn't hesitate for a second."

"Hmm. Going AWOL... Not a very good idea at the best of times."

"I know, but then I just didn't care. I knew there was a chance you would not make it. I was stuck over there not knowing and it was driving me nuts."

"You had a job to do."

Kate looked intently at Tyler, gave a little shrug, and grinned.

"Yes. I did. So I made pancakes for everyone."

Tyler's eyes sparkled in the moonlight.

She smiled, delighted.

"Really?" she said.

"Yep. Used up all your stash, and I got the entire platoon together. We had pancakes and Starbucks coffee and toasted you and Ben. And that is the only thing about that day which is really worth remembering," Kate concluded before looking far out to sea once more.

Tyler gazed at her for a moment, and then she kissed her on the lips, very softly.

"Thank you," she said.

"For what?"

"Taking care of my guys. Taking care of me."

"Nasty business but someone's got to do it," Kate remarked with pretend seriousness.

She enjoyed the smile on Tyler's lips as her lover laughed quietly.

"Hey, babe. Are you feeling better now?"

"Yes. Much."

"You think you can go back to bed and sleep this time? It would

do you a world of good."
"I know. Will you stay with me?"
Kate's reply was simple and true.
"Always," she said.

The End

STRONG

STRONG

NATALIE DEBRABANDERE